CENTRE STAGE

REBEL ROCK BOOK 1

SUSAN HARRIS

A Note From The Author

Music has always been a huge part of my life so it was only natural that it leaked into my stories. When it came to Heartache Melody I knew that I wanted their songs to be truly original.

All of the original songs found in Centre Stage, and any of the Rebel Universe stories, written by Heartache Melody, are in fact original songs written by me, with the help of Melanie from Melanie's Muses.

I hope you hear them in your head the way we heard them in ours.

PROLOGUE

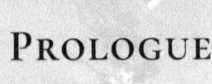

Andrea

THE SOUND of a guitar being strummed echoed through the halls as Andrea made her way down to the music room where her brother Rhys and his bandmate Declan Walsh practiced. Andrea had spent most of the afternoon sorting flyers for her brother and his best friend while they held auditions for band members, keeping herself busy so she didn't stress about the fact that tonight, she would be all alone with the guy she had been crushing on for years.

Declan Walsh was funny, smart, a homebody like her and she loved spending hours sharing music with him. While she and Declan were the same age, it was Rhys who had introduced them, having met at a music

3

lesson and they became firm friends when Declan helped him learn how to read sheet music, finding a way to help Rhys who was dyslexic.

They were due to see a band that she and Declan liked, but Rhys wasn't keen on, so tonight was the night she was going to be brave and tell Declan how she felt, hoping that the secret smiles and the flirty touches were not all in her head.

Taking a deep breath, Andrea put her hand on the door, then hesitated when she heard Rhys say. "Dude, this thing with my sister...it's not like a date is it?"

Her heart was beating so loud inside her chest that she almost didn't hear Declan's answer. Her stomach dropped the moment she heard him let loose a chortle of laughter.

"Seriously? Andi? Your ballbusting, take no prisoner's sister?" Declan said with a whistle through his teeth. "Are you insane?"

Andrea clutched the flyers to her chest, tears welling as she struggled to take in air. Had she been imagining the chemistry between them? Had it all been a ruse?

"Phew." Andrea heard Rhys chuckle before he said. "Ya, cause, if you ended up dating my sister that would have been all kinds of weird."

"For sure." Declan agreed as he played with the strings of his guitar like he had played with the strings of her heart. "And when we are famous rock stars, we're gonna have women throwing themselves at us.

No one wants a ball and chain at seventeen. I'll go to the gig since the ticket is free, but me and Andi? Never gonna happen."

Andrea felt a sob clawing at her throat as she heard the boys finishing up and she bolted, taking off down the hall, tossing the flyers in the bin as she ran out of the school and promised never to let her heart be so foolish ever again.

Declan Walsh would rue the day he thought he was better than her.

CHAPTER ONE

Andrea

SIX YEARS later

Andrea "Andi" Collins strode around her and her best friend Charlie's apartment, making sure she had all her bits and pieces sorted before she flew home to Ireland tomorrow. The thought of going home made her both anxious, and excited. She loved her family and friends, but the chance she would run into Declan Walsh while at home was massive.

It had been six years since she had told her parents she wanted to go abroad to study, six years since she stood Declan up at the gig they were going to because Andi had overheard her teenage crush basically slating her. Andi had been so in love with the dark-haired, devastating smiled handsome teen that seeing him every day after that would have been torture.

Andi had always been smart, found it easy to learn anything, and her parents had been only too happy to let her go to a private school for the last few months and then to apply to the university in Manchester to study PR, specializing in music.

Music had always been a passion for her, and she could have been in a band herself, but she had decided not to venture down the girl band route and instead, focus on making sure others' dreams came true.

And it was at that university in Manchester that Andi had crossed paths with Charlotte Coyle and once they realized they were the only two Irish girls in the course, they quickly bonded. Charlie was the opposite of Andi: Charlie was sporty, shy with those she didn't know, and a disaster when it came to fashion, but when Andi had walked in on the first day and heard Charlie talking on the phone, they had immediately clicked.

Andi walked into the lecture hall, glancing around almost relieved when she noticed she was one of the first few people to arrive. There was a small group of girls up the back who looked like they had known each other for years, one of them had hair a brash colour of red that had Andi rolling her eyes.

There was a solitary girl a few rows from the front who was talking on the phone and Andi's ear caught the Cork accent right off.

"Da, I'm grand. I promise. I'm moving into the dorm later."

The girl was smiling, her eyes twinkling as she shook her head and lowered her voice. "Da, I'm good. And no, I want to experience college like a normal person. I gotta go. I love you."

The girl hung up her phone and looked up, her eyes meeting Andi's, a faint blush on her cheeks. Andi strode forward and grinned. "They don't stop being your parents just cause you leave the country, do they?"

The girl blinked in surprise then returned Andi's grin. "Oh my God, you dunno how nice it is to hear a familiar accent!"

Andi slid into the seat beside her, holding out her hand. "Andi Collins."

The girl took her hand. "Charlie Coyle."

Dropping her hand, Andi nudged her shoulder and said. "You and me, Charlie. We are gonna be the best of friends. I just know it."

They had been inseparable since, her and Charlie, ending up sharing a dorm room like it was fate, bonding over dickhead first crushes, and plotting and planning to take over the world and open Rebel PR. They had managed to do so, with a little investment by Charlie's millionaire dad, his race car company quickly making strides and last year they had finally entered F1.

The company had been so successful in its first year that she and Charlie had decided to open an Irish branch to cope with the influx of clients. And now that Charlie's dad had sadly passed away and left Charlie his multi-million company, Charlie would have less time to devote to the business they had cultivated and Andi couldn't be in two places at once.

Her friend had returned home to Cork to begin her life as CEO of her dad's company and face the demons of her past. Charlie was most apprehensive about seeing rising racing star Noah Donovan, and Andi could totally understand exactly how Charlie must be feeling.

Andi knew because that was exactly how she felt. Going home meant seeing her family and her brother and where Rhys was, Declan tended to be. Their band had taken off recently, like Andi always knew they would and they were a hot commodity, trying to finish the last few tracks of their debut album.

She spoke to Rhys nearly every day and if they weren't calling, they were texting. They had been close growing up, with a mere eleven months between them and they had always been a musical family. Their dad played for fun in a trad group, playing the bodhrán of all things. Rhys played the guitar and the keyboard, and Andi did too.

But while Rhys couldn't sing worth a damn, Andi loved to sing and she did as often as she could, especially after a few pints during open mic night at the college bar she had worked during college to support herself

Charlie came and sat with her most nights she

tended bar despite the fact she didn't have to work for cash. Charlie never made her feel like she was poor or offered her money when she was short because she knew Andrea would ask if she needed help She respected Andi's need to work for the things she had and Andi worked her ass off so she could be an equal partner in Rebel PR.

She loved the bones off Charlie, like she was the best friend she'd always wanted growing up. When she was a teenager, she had felt so different to the girls in her school, hadn't gelled with anyone of her own sex and when she told her mam that, wise as always Mabel Collins told her.

"Sometimes, you have to wait a little longer in life to find the person who is the other half of your soul. And I don't mean a romantic soulmate, I mean the other person who you know has your back without question. The person you would call if you needed to bury a body."

Her mam was as funny as she was wise sometimes.

Striding over to the fridge, Andi took out a bottle of beer, opening it and curling her legs under herself before she decided to give Charlie a call and see how her friend was coping being back on Irish soil.

The phone rang a few times before Andi heard a welcome voice on the other end.

"I haven't even been in Ireland five minutes and you can't cope without me."

That made Andi grin as she sipped her beer. "Darling, you have no idea. I am so ready to head home tomorrow and see you. That new intern spilled coffee all over the soccer star who just got called up to the first team for England and then insulted him by stating she never understood why professional footballers got paid so much to kick a damn ball. Fucking idiot."

Charlie laughed so hard that it made Andi laugh as well, easing some of the tension in her stomach. Andi was about to ask Charlie if she was okay when Charlie said. "Andi, I'm about to pull up at the house. Are you sure you don't want to stay here for the few days?"

While Andi was tempted, and tempted she definitely was, her little rental would do while she looked for a base in Ireland. Her mam and dad had been a little miffed that she wouldn't stay with them but Andi said she would be coming and going at all hours so it was best she stayed elsewhere.

"Nah, girl, I'm all good." She reassured her friend. "I think you'll have enough on your plate being all boss bitch to he who shall not be named. I have the meeting with the boys from the band the record company want me to manage and that interview you wanted me to sit in on but we defo need pints afterward. See ya in a few days, biatch."

They hung up and Andi sipped her beer, gazing out the window at Manchester illuminated by a vast array of lights and Andi wondered if it would be possible for her to go home and have her meeting in two days for the record company and manage to avoid seeing Declan at any cost.

It had taken six months of ignoring his calls, his texts, the voice notes he had left asking why she had blown him off and left him standing outside the gig by himself for Declan to get the hint and leave her alone. The only thing Andi could do was put an ocean between her and Declan to mend her broken heart.

But her feelings for Declan Walsh were long forgotten...

And that was one of the many lies Andi told herself.

Chapter Two

Andrea

Andrea's week was not going well.

Not only had her flight been delayed due to high winds, her luggage had been lost and the dickhead at the customer service desk had pissed her off so much that Andrea had been about to reach over the counter and smack his head off the desk when Rhys had shown up to collect her and with one smile from her brother, the starstruck man had offered to track down Andrea's luggage.

So the time she was meant to be relaxing and preparing for her big meeting had been spent rushing around cork city to try and get some work-appropriate clothes. She even had to borrow Rhys's car to get around because Nicolette had flaked and hadn't bothered to get her a rental.

And of course the moment she and Rhys were in the same proximity, they reverted to teenagers again, with Andrea commenting on the stink of alcohol when she hugged Rhys and then when Rhys asked her to come out with him and the band, they had argued when Andrea retorted that she was happy to go out with the band if Declan stayed at home.

Rhys hadn't been happy that Andrea was clinging to her grudge against his best friend, especially when Andrea refused to tell him why she had suddenly started to despise Declan.

As Andrea drove to her meeting at the city centre hotel, she passed the school that they had all gone to and it made her think back to the absolute torture that had made her leave school after she had overheard Declan slating her to her brother all those years ago.

It had been horrible walking into school after she had ghosted Declan at the concert and ignored his messages all weekend. She had managed to avoid him the entire midterm break as well. The calls, the texts, even him showing up at her house and her mam telling the boy who had a key to their front door that Andi wasn't in, had all come to a sudden stop, and when Andrea returned to school, her torment had begun.

A shoulder collided with hers and Andrea went crashing into her locker with a grunt. Whirling round, Andrea let loose a slew of curses as she turned to see

Lauren Smyth smirking at her. She swept her long blonde hair off her shoulder and pursed her glossed lips as she cocked her hip, her gaggle of mindless bimbos behind her.

"You really should watch where you're going, Andrea."

"Be careful yourself, Lauren." Andrea tossed back, looking down at the petite girl. "or next time you'll end up walking into my fist."

Lauren snickered, rolling her eyes. "You always were all talk, Andrea. You wouldn't dare."

Andrea clenched her fists and tried to rein in her temper. Her and Lauren had been at odds for years, going back to early on in First Year when Andrea beat Lauren to get the main part in the play and Lauren had to settle for a secondary role. It had boosted Andrea's popularity, even for an outcast like her.

And they used to be on friendly terms...not friends...but not enemies like they were now.

"What's going on here, babe?"

For one electrifying moment, when Andrea heard the voice, she thought that Declan was talking about her. But no, the object of her affection and the person who had broken her heart into smithereens slung his muscular arm around Lauren's shoulders and lifted his electric blue eyes to clash with Andrea's.

Lauren snuggled into his arms, her smirk deepening as she took stock of Andrea's obvious shock and the way Declan allowed Lauren to slip her fingers into his.

"Andi's being mean to me."

"Well, Andi needs to mind her fucking manners."

Their eyes never moved from one another's, the tension almost tight enough to snap and then Declan shifted his gaze and brushed his lips over Lauren's hair.

"Ignore her, babe. She doesn't matter in the slightest, a few weeks left in this hellhole and no one will even remember her. Let's go."

Declan nudged Lauren away and her crew followed after her like the little sheep they were. Andrea sagged against her locker, aware that everyone in the school had gathered to witness the way that the most popular guy in school had publicly shunned her.

Andrea shifted her gaze to where Declan was striding away with Lauren tucked under his arm and then, as if he knew, Declan cast a glance over his shoulder and if looks could kill, Andrea would be a bloody mess on the halls of the school.

A car beeped its horn at her and she realized the light that she had stopped at had changed. Andrea accelerated, driving into the underground car park and took a minute to catch her breath before she got out of the car and reminded herself that she was no longer that Andrea, but Andi Collins - a successful business-woman who had secured deals with million-euro foot-ballers and called Hollywood heartthrobs her friends.

But this was the major big time...Emerald Records had called her and asked her to exclusively handle all the PR and media for their newest band and that excited Andrea more than she cared to admit. With everything that had happened with Declan, Andrea had pushed aside her love for music and gone down other avenues but now this was her chance to reclaim what Declan's actions had stripped from her.

When they had planned on going to the concert, Andrea was planning on telling Declan that she had gone to an audition and was about to sign a contract that would make her a star. She had never told Declan she could sing, had been too embarrassed to sing in front of him because it felt too raw, made her feel exposed.

But then everything went to hell and the record company wanted Andrea to be in a girl group and all Andrea could remember was Declan, Rhys, and Jameson taking the piss out of the manufactured pop groups that were suddenly appearing on the TV and how shite they were.

It was what had made Andrea turn down the record deal and decide that she needed an entire ocean between her and Declan. It had been hard, leaving her family and starting over but doing so had sent her directly in the path of Charlie Coyle and their bond was unbreakable.

A small thin man waited at the door of the hotel, his designer suit all sleek and shiny as he ran his gaze over her and Andrea plastered on her best fake smile, ignoring the urge to punch the rich jackass square in the jaw.

"Andrea Collins," Tim Brett drawled, his eyes running over her a second time. "it's so lovely to finally see you in person. You look as stunning as you do on TV."

Andrea had been to a few premiers with JJ, a rising movie pin-up and it had gotten her more attention than the time she had run the gauntlet amid a soccer star scandal.

"It's nice to meet you in person too." Andrea lied her ass off because this guy had her future in his hands and if they landed this contract, it would be the first major deal for the Irish office of Rebel PR. "I've got loads of ideas and contacts so am ready to meet the band."

Part of the deal was that Andrea had no idea who this shit hot band was until the big reveal and Andrea hated surprises. Tim held opened the door, steering her inside as he chatted away about how much Emerald Records was excited to have an Irish manager who would understand the homegrown talent and getting their album finished and marketed.

Andrea smiled and nodded as Tim led her up the elevator to the penthouse and as the door opened and she heard the faint strumming of a guitar and the clinking of glasses. Apparently, the band had decided to start the party early, and long before she had arrived.

"This partnership is going to put both Emerald Records and Rebel PR on the radar of all the right people. I think this will be the start of a beautiful relationship and we will all end up being one big happy family."

Andrea gave Tim a faint smile as she stepped into the penthouse and her heart dropped to her stomach as the band turned around to look at her and all but one of the members looked shocked to see her.

But it was the man strumming the guitar that had anger igniting her veins as Declan Walsh, lead singer of Heartache Melody held her gaze and it was like she was seventeen all over again and her heart was being ripped from her chest.

Her douchebag brother grinned so wide she wanted to deck him. "Surprise!"

Andrea folded her arms across her chest, glaring at Declan as she said. "You have got to be fucking kidding me."

CHAPTER THREE

Declan

"YOU HAVE GOT to be fucking kidding me."

That acerbic bite in Andi Collins tone ripped through Declan like he had been shot, the sudden impact of seeing her when he hadn't been prepared made his fingers stumble over the chords. Her gorgeous face was marred by an annoyed frown, her lips pursed to emphasize just how pissed she really was. Her arms folded across her chest pushed her round breasts up and Declan had to concentrate real hard not to let his gaze linger on her cleavage.

Andi Collins was five foot eight with long lean legs, curves that made Declan think of what it would be like to get his hands on them, and even as a horny teenage boy he had wanted to run his fingers through her caramel-coloured hair. Her eyes reminded him of top-shelf whiskey and he had always wanted to get lost in her, even way back then.

Until it had all gone horribly wrong.

Tim looked worried as he glanced at Rhys and Declan would be having a word with him the moment the record executive was out of earshot. Rhys staggered forward, grinning like the dope he was as he went to hug his sister and Andi side-stepped him, the idiot almost losing his balance.

It would serve him right if he face-planted in front of all the record people.

"I was assured by Mr. Collins that Rebel PR was the right company to handle all of Heartache Melody's dealings. Perhaps this was a mistake."

Declan's stomach rolled as he wondered if Rhys had blown this for the band but Andi unfolded her arms and touched her hand to Tim's arm with a fake ass warm smile that still had Declan wanting to rip Andi's hand from the slimy guy's arm.

"It's no big deal. My brother just has a weird sense of humour. I'm sure if there is any conflict of interest that I can have one of my capable staff take over with the day-to-day management."

Declan set the guitar aside and got to his feet, with Andi snapping her gaze to him.

"There's no conflict of interest. It's Andi or no one." Declan heard himself say in a tone that had both Jameson Kent and Luna Sullivan looking at him with raised brows.

Tim clapped his hands and started to talk to Andi about studio time, going to London to record the album and all the appearances that they could line up for the band. Declan listened intently as Andi turned to Tim. "Declan has built a perfectly good studio here in Cork where the band feels at home. I think that having a home-grown Irish band record their debut album from their hand-built studio would only add to the appeal."

Declan almost grinned with the knowledge that Andi knew enough about the band to know they wanted to finish recording the album where the band had started. At the start it had been just him and Rhys, then Jameson had joined when Declan persuaded his next-door neighbour after hearing him shredding a guitar.

They had held open auditions for a drummer and the moment the fiery red-haired Luna Sullivan had sat down behind Declan's second-hand drum kit and burst into *Arctic Monkeys 'brainstorm'*, Declan knew he wasn't letting the girl walk out the door. The girl couldn't hold a note but she was a powerhouse on the drums.

He might have been shocked that Andi was going to be managing them and he hated to admit it but Rhys had been dead on with his choice. He had spent countless hours talking music and ideas with Andi on the floor of Rhys' bedroom or staring at the stars out her parent's back garden. Andi loved music as much as he did, played a little too so it made sense to have someone who knew them watching their back.

Didn't mean that working alongside the woman who had ghosted him without so much as a reason would be easy. She hadn't even bothered to offer an explanation before she just wasn't in school anymore leaving Declan to find out from Rhys that Andi was leaving Ireland to study in the UK.

As Tim went to answer a phone call, Andi introduced herself to Luna, since they had never met in person, and then she hugged Jameson and asked how his nan was doing. They chatted for a few minutes until Rhys came over and slung an arm around his sister, who promptly elbowed him in the stomach.

Luna was grilling Andi about her life in Manchester and if she was really on such friendly terms with Joshua James and had she seen him naked. Andi laughed and shook her head and something loosened in Declan as he heard Andi say she didn't have time for a relationship, because she was too busy being the boss.

Andi must have sensed him watching her, because she peered over her shoulder, the barest hint of insecurity in her eyes before it vanished and she turned back to the other members of the band.

They had avoided each other for years after he had admittedly been a colossal dickhead and dated an airhead just to get back at her for standing him up. They had been planning to see a concert and he had practised what he wanted to say to Andi for weeks, finally telling her that he was in love with her and she had blown him off.

It had hurt like a muthafucker to have his heart broken.

Declan stood under the entrance of the nightclub, waiting for Andi to arrive. She was late and Andrea Collins was never late to meet up with him. He had texted her a few times telling her he was excited for the gig and couldn't wait to see her, but it was forty-five minutes after they were supposed to meet and Andi hadn't shown.

He sent her a few texts to ask was she late but got nothing in return. Declan had been teased by his three younger brothers, the triplets, because he had even brushed his unruly hair and put on some aftershave. His Ma had shooed the demon children away and patted him on the cheek telling him to go with his heart.

And his heart was telling him Andi was it for him.

It was sappy and stupid for an eighteen year old to be thinking like that, but his Ma had met and married his Da by nineteen and they were blissfully happy until his Da had died in a fire while working, leaving his Ma with Declan and the triplets all under ten years old.

Declan shook thoughts of his Da out of his mind as he pulled out his phone and called Andi, only to be told that the customer had her phone switched off. Declan called Rhys instead, his best friend answering on the second ring.

"Deco, what's up?"

"You any idea when your sister is going to arrive for the gig. I'm freezing my balls off here."

Rhys didn't laugh in response, just sighed and replied. "Deco, she's not coming mate."

"What do you mean, Rhys? Where is she?"

"Listen, mate, I'm not getting in between it. Andi came home from school and just said she never wanted to speak to you again and that was the end of it. I'm sorry, Deco. I don't have a clue what's wrong."

Declan hung up the phone, anger bubbling inside his chest as he typed out an angry message, telling Andi just how he felt and that if she couldn't be bothered to show up or be upfront with him then she wasn't the girl she thought.

But despite the anger in him, Declan erased the message and hailed a cab, heading for the party that the sixth class was having at Lauren Smyth's house so he could drink himself to oblivion and forget about Andrea fucking Collins.

Her laughter now at something Jameson said to her irked him, he felt the muscle in his jaw tick as Andrea asked Jameson how opposed he was to a tasteful half-naked photoshoot. Luna grinned and said she was all in and when Rhys commented that he was happy to get naked, Andi rolled her eyes and snorted. "Everyone's already seen your skinny ass before Rhys. No one's gonna pay for that, bro."

Rhys just laughed at his sister as Tim came in and asked was everything all right. Andi grinned and said that she was happy to manage the band and guaranteed that the album would be ready by the deadline even if she had to lock them all in the studio to get it finished.

Tim was barely out of the penthouse when Declan stalked toward Andi, unable to reign in his temper and he knew he'd need a sparring session with Noah soon. He grabbed Andi's arm and growled. "We need to talk. Alone. Now!"

CHAPTER FOUR

Andrea

"TAKE YOUR HAND OFF ME, Declan Walsh or I swear I'll deck ya." Andrea hissed as she jerked her hand out of Declan's grasp like he had burned her. Her heart was racing, the fact that Declan was glowering at her excited her more than she cared to admit but there was no doubt to anyone in the room that whatever was going on between them was combustible.

Rhys waited until Declan had removed his hand then he stepped between the two of them, forcing each of them to take a step back. Andrea shook her head with a frustrated sigh but it was Rhys who spoke to try and diffuse the situation.

"I think everyone needs to stall on for a second and

calm down. If I knew that me pitching the idea of having Andi as our manager was going to be this bad, I'd have kept my mouth shut."

"There's no issue, Rhys," Declan growled, scrubbing a hand down his beard and stubble. "I just need to have a few words with Andi. Alone."

Rhys looked at her and Andi smiled. "It's all good, Rhys. I have a few things I need to sort with Declan before I get stuck into making you guys the biggest names in Irish rock."

She offered a quick goodbye to the rest of the band, taking Luna's details with the promise she would call her to arrange a girl's night. Rhys passed by her, his pierced eyebrow raised as if to question whether or not Andrea was cool with being left alone with Declan.

"I'll see you at home tonight. Mam has ordered me to dinner 'cause I work too hard and don't eat enough home-cooked meals."

Rhys laughed, shaking his head, holding out his fist to bump Declan's before he left, closing the door behind him and leaving her alone with Declan.

Gone was the boy with the stubble and the killer smile and now, standing before her, was the rock god the Irish media had started to call him. A thick beard covered his face and framed his full lips, the dark brown strands of his hair falling into his eyes, eyes that were dark and intelligent and entirely focused on her.

"I'm sure we can find a way to work amicably with one another. We can keep things professional." Andrea said, folding her arms across her chest, and damn if it didn't send a thrill through her at the way his eyes dipped for a split second before returning to her face.

"Sure we can. Just depends if you are gonna cut and run on us like you did years ago."

Andrea felt the rage simmering in her veins so she closed her eyes and counted to five before she lifted her lashes. "This is strictly business. If you succeed, then Rebel PR succeeds. I have a vested interest in making sure that you go global. We may not like one another, Declan, but I am a consummate professional who hates to fail. I don't intend to let out childish, petty differences get in the way of making us a hell of a lot of money."

A muscle in Declan's jaw ticked as he folded his arms across his broad chest to mimic her own stance, holding her gaze. He opened his mouth to retort then closed it, then opened it again.

"We need to sit down and discuss where you intend to take the band. We need to see if your vision lines up with what we have in mind."

Andrea felt her shoulders relax as the tension eased because this was a safe topic for them to discuss. "That sounds like a plan. I'll be spending some time in Cork before I have to return for a few events in Manchester that only I can handle. I would love to sit down with the band and go through ideas I have. I want to get you guys more exposure. More eyes and ears because the moment the right song clicks, that's it, Heartache Melody will be on everyone's playlist."

She heard the excitement in her own voice, and saw the surprise in Declan's eyes as he regarded her. "You and me can meet next week and go through the plan. Then, if our ideas line up, we can bring them to the rest of the band."

Andrea was so taken aback by his suggestion that she barked out a laugh. "I'd rather spend the afternoon working with the band and getting a head start on things. I'll come by the studio in the next few days and we can all hash out ideas."

"Afraid to be alone with me, Andi?" Declan's lips curved into a smug smile but Andrea was quick to give as good as Declan was giving her.

"Time is money, Declan. No point wasting time with just you when I have the whole band to manage. Heartache Melody is not just you."

Heat flared in his gaze as Declan shook his head and went to collect his guitar. It was the same one that he'd had as a teenager, the old acoustic like a comfort blanket that Declan carried everywhere with him even though he had a collection of guitars in his studio.

"Make sure to stop by and visit me ma while you're here. She would knife me if she knew you were back in Cork and hadn't called in for a cuppa."

There had been so much animosity between them over the years that Andrea was surprised at the warmth in Declan's tone. Just like he had spent hours in her house, both Andrea and Rhys had spent a considerable amount of time in Declan's family home, and Andrea had even tried to babysit the terror triplets with Declan.

Andrea smiled, knowing that Mrs. Walsh would indeed chastise her eldest son if he didn't make her go round one of the days she was here. "I'll pop round someday. Check to make sure the triplets are keeping out of trouble."

Declan snorted as he zipped up his guitar case. "Chance would be a fine thing." Then the warmth left his tone as he straightened. "We will be at the studio all next week putting some melody behind lyrics to see if a song works. Come by and we can get started."

Andrea shifted back into business mode. "Absolutely. I want to get to grips with what we need to do before I head back to Manchester just before Christmas. I have a few things to sort and then I should be in Ireland for the most part once January comes."

"Won't the movie star care that his arm candy is in another country?" Declan tossed at her, a growl in his tone.

Andrea brushed her hair off her shoulder. "Not that it's any of your business but JJ is just a friend. Men and women can be friends without there being anything going on." Andrea let her lips kick up into a grin. "Besides, his private jet can pick me up whenever he needs me."

"Don't make yourself sound cheap, Andi."

Oh hell, that statement pissed her off.

"Fuck you, Declan. If I want to wear an expensive dress and walk a red carpet with a Hollywood star, that's my decision and you can shove your outdated views up your arse. It's called networking, and whether it's a premiere, or a dinner with a sports star or a politician, *I* decide what I do. Both myself and Charlie schmooze with clients for the advancement of Rebel PR and I will do the same so that Heartache Melody succeeds. So, if that bothers you, the next time you see me walk my fine ass down the red carpet, turn off the goddamn TV."

Andrea whirled on her heels, ignoring the way Declan growled her name as she walked said fine ass out the door and into the lift, hoping the SOB watched her walk away. How dare he cheapen her down to that level, like she hadn't worked hard to be as good as she was. For fuck sake, how the hell did he still have the ability to rile her up so much.

Because you still have feelings for him...

Pushing that thought to the back of her mind, Andrea headed down to grab Rhys' car so she could head back to her rental and relax for the afternoon while she went over contracts, and hopefully, she could call up Charlie and vent to her about their mutual dislike for beautiful boys who had broken their hearts.

Andrea made her way down to the carpark, scanning to try and find Rhys's car that wasn't where she had parked it. Andrea frowned, reaching into her handbag for the keys but failing to find them and Andrea knew in that moment that her brother had swiped the keys and left her stranded and angry.

"Son of a bitch!" Andrea screamed in frustration but she knew somewhere in Cork city, her brother was busting a gut laughing.

CHAPTER FIVE

Declan

DECLAN HAD MADE it home under a haze of anger and jealousy unable to stop himself from thinking about Andi's anger fuelled statement when he had let his jealousy rule the voice in his head that was telling him to shut the hell up instead of making the already volatile situation worse. He'd had the opportunity to start off peacefully, but instead, he had pulled the pin on the grenade that was him and Andi.

"So if that bothers you, the next time you see me walk my fine ass down the red carpet, turn off the goddamn TV."

And of course as Andi strode out of the penthouse, all Declan could do was dip his eyes to said fine ass before she disappeared from view and he had to take a few minutes to rein himself in before he left the penthouse and headed for his apartment.

He had fallen in love with the space as soon as he saw it while helping Luna's dad clear it out. It was a two-story warehouse that he felt could be turned into a studio on the ground floor and an apartment for him upstairs. It had stone walls and concrete floors that just had called to him and once all the paperwork was signed and sealed, his three brothers, the band, and even Luke and Noah had come to help him sort out both the studio and the apartment.

He had worked his fair share of dead-end jobs in order to be able to afford his warehouse in the south side of the city. Luna's dad had been looking to sell the place after the tenants moved out and he had sold it to Declan for a steal under the stipulation that the band didn't forget that it was Mike who had given the band their very first gig in the family-run bar.

Declan loved Luna and her twin brother Luke's father. He worked hard to make sure his kids got the chance to live their dreams but making sure they stayed grounded, just like his Ma did. Luke and Luna were still expected to pull their weight and tend the bar when they could, even if Luke was always busy considering he was an F1 race car driver.

Jogging up the stairs to the open-plan apartment, Declan tossed his keys to the side, set his guitar down beside the couch, then opened the fridge and pulled out a beer before he threw himself down on the sofa and pulled his phone out of his pocket to call Noah. Luke had introduced Declan to Noah, his teammate and rising star in single-seater racing years ago and they had hit it off right from the first moment. Then Noah had asked the band to play at his twenty-first birthday party and that was when people really started to take notice of Heartache Melody, and doors had started to open.

But other than that, Noah was sound. He hadn't had the best childhood, to be fair. And like Declan, Noah had a history with a girl who he couldn't let go of no matter how much he tried.

It was just the universe's karma that the two women in question were his Andi and Charlotte Coyle, Noah's new boss at Rebel Racers.

And when the fuck did he start calling Andi his again?

Rolling his eyes, Declan pressed call and didn't even wait for the other man to say hello before he grunted out. "I've had one hell of a morning...how's your girl?"

Noah's response came immediately down the phone in a pissed-off tone. "She's not my girl and so far, I've been avoiding her."

Noah wasn't one to run from a fight, had been fighting his whole life to chase his dreams, and yet, there was something about Charlotte Coyle that had the cocky git behaving like a shy, surly teen again. But, hey, who was he to judge considering he defaulted to grouchy asshole mode the moment Andi had stepped into the room.

He had been avoiding the past and what had happened between him and Andi like the plague for years, pouring his anger into lyrics and music, and a hell of a lot of alcohol.

"Noah," Declan said with a sigh, "if today has taught me anything, ya can't run from your past man. That fucker will sucker punch you when you least expect it. Go and get it over with and then meet me in O'Malley's for a pint."

Declan hung up the phone, knowing Noah would meet him at the bar and they could put the world to rights without the pressure of having the band around. O'Malley's was a little firefighter pub his Da used to take him to and he was always welcomed there when he stopped by. Normally they would go to Luna and Luke's dad's pub but sometimes, he and Noah just wanted to sit and talk shite and not have the band around them.

Noah didn't judge him for all the stupid shit he had done before Andi left to go to college nor did Declan judge Noah for what he had done to push Charlie away. They kept each other's confidence, knowing the other would never, ever divulge any secrets.

Declan ran his fingers through his hair before he allowed himself to think back to the last massive fight he and Andi had before she left school to spend the last few months of her leaving cert in private study.

They had been clashing for weeks, Declan's girlfriend Lauren having it in for Andi and because Declan had been so angry at Andi, he had let it happen. He had treated her so badly because he was hurt, and he had let his ego rule his actions.

The door to the music room burst open and Andi came rushing in like a hurricane. Her cheeks were flushed with her temper and her eyes showed the hurt and the pain that their recent clashes had caused.

"You bastard!" Andi snarled at him, striding forward with her fists clenched. "how dare you show that loose knickered bitch the lyrics I helped you write and then tell her it was my way of throwing myself at you. She plastered the lyrics all over my locker. Do you have to humiliate me in every way possible?"

Declan shrugged his shoulders, trying to appear nonchalant when in fact he was dying a little inside. He hadn't even shown Lauren the damn lyrics. She had snooped in his lyric book, songs that he and Andi had worked on and when Lauren had laughed at some of it, Declan had told her the lyrics were all Andi.

He hadn't expected Lauren to go and be as vindictive as she had been and now, without his knowledge, his personal lyrics and feelings were all over the school, even if they were blaming Andi. And he hadn't told anyone otherwise.

He'd already fallen out with Rhys because of it, and

now Andi was standing in front of him looking shattered.

"I can't do it anymore. I can't deal. You've won, Declan. You've fucking won."

That was one of the last times he had seen Andi in person alone and he had sat there like a lemon and said nothing. The lyrics had been deeply personal to them both, writing like it was a duet, with him singing both parts and it had been less angsty, less rock than he was used to but it was his and Andi's lyrics.

They had spent hours lying on the floor of Rhys's bedroom and trying to perfect it but they never got around to finishing it. It remained unfinished in one of his many lyric books because he couldn't bring himself to conclude without her.

Instead, he had written songs about her that he would never sing to her. Songs that were filled with pain and anger and regret. Some he had tested with the band to see if they worked toward the album and others were just so deep and raw he couldn't share with anyone and he tweaked those in the midnight hours alone in the studio where no one could see into his soul.

He had tried to talk to her when her parents threw her a leaving party but she had evaded him all evening. And then she was gone along with his hopes of making amends, of coming clean and finding out why she had not turned up at the concert that night.

But now Andi was back and would be staying in Cork for the foreseeable future.

It was up to him to take the opportunity to have his say and to get closure on one of the most important things in his life so maybe he could move on with his life and forget that he was still in love with Andi Collins after all this time.

And maybe he was just fucking kidding himself.

CHAPTER SIX

Andrea

ANDREA WAVED off the woman at the reception of Rebel Racers as she offered to escort her to Charlie's office, the woman frowning as Andrea simply headed up the stairs. She could see Charlie on a call, her friend gesturing with her free hand. Andrea grinned as she knocked at the door, then sauntered in just as Charlie finished up.

The first thing she did was hug Charlie and apologize for not turning up days ago like she planned. "I'm so sorry I'm a few days late but we seriously need shots to toast an end to this nightmare week!"

Andi all but threw herself down on a chair, dangling

her legs off the side as she whinged to Charlie. "Of all the bands Emerald Records wants me to do PR for, it had to be Heartache Melody. Apparently, when they found out that I was Rhys' sister, they decided it would be perrrrrrfect for me to run with it. Fuck my life."

"So seeing the rock god again went as well as my first interaction with Noah went?"

Andi sighed, not wanting to go into the boy drama especially since she was debating whether or not to tell Charlie that she had a run-in with Noah Donovan herself a few days ago over their phone and their interaction had gone anything but smooth.

"Um well, you don't sound like Charlie?" Andrea mused down the phone at the gruff but sexy tone.

"She's not here, can I take a message?" the voice barked down the line and Andrea was sure she recognised it.

She was wondering if the person answering the phone was the same man who had broken her best friend's heart and decided to push some buttons. "Oh, leave it to Charlie to only be in her office all of five minutes and hire herself an assistant with a sexy radio voice."

"You want me to take a message or not? I don't have time for the verbal banter."

Andrea felt her own temper flare, sucked in a breath, then went into full-out boss bitch tone. "I don't know who you think you are talking to with that tone, but please let me know your name so I can tell your boss, my business partner which asshole to fire.

There was no hesitation as Mr. Smartass told her. "Sweetheart, my contract is so ironclad that even Charlie can't break it. So, the names Noah, Noah Donovan, if you want to try and get Charlie to hand me my pink slip. Or do you just want me to pass on that you called? You could try her mobile."

"Like I didn't try that already smartass." Andrea snorted, rolling her eyes at the idiot on the other end of the line retorted. "I can see it's going to be fucking picnic working with you, Noah Donovan."

Charlotte ordered two americanos then said as she leaned back in her seat. "You can hand this off to Nicolette if you want."

Andrea knew Charlie was looking out for her, but if Charlie had the balls to work alongside Noah all day, then Andrea could do the same with Declan. She rolled her eyes. "I love Nicolette but the chances of her dropping her knickers if any of the lads even show the slightest interest could tank the relationship. Leave her to handle that girl band reunion and keep her out of trouble and the headlines."

They both knew their college classmate would cause mayhem in Ireland so that was the end of that conversation.

"So, before you argue with me, Charlie, I'm in major need of some dancing, some vodka, and a dirty munch when the club closes outside the fountain."

"Andi," Charlotte groaned, shaking her head, making Andrea grin. "You know I can't just rock up to a bar right now without bringing the Irish media trailing after me."

A knock sounded on the door and Luke Sullivan walked in all Irish smiles and ginger hair. "I was passing by and said I would drop these in." Luke set the coffees down on the desk before he turned to Andrea with a boyish smile that Andrea had no doubt made girls swoon.

"Luke Sullivan."

"I had the pleasure of meeting your twin a couple of days ago."

Luke shook his head as he laughed. "Should I apologies for the fact my sister has no filter in advance?"

"She's definitely a straight shooter, your sister. But then again, she has to put up with my brother so..."

Luke's eyes widened. "No way! Your Rhys' Andi?"

"For my sins."

Like the fact that they both had this newfound connection because of their siblings, Andrea chatted away to Luke about the band, his family, and even his bar, Luke smiling when Andrea told him she was a dab hand at tending bar herself. Then Luke told her that a few people were getting together at his dad's bar and it would be totally private.

Andrea could see Charlie lost in her thoughts. "We would love to, wouldn't we, Charlie?"

"Umm sure..." Charlie said noncommittedly, her cheeks pinking with embarrassment at being caught out so Andrea gave her a mischievous smile.

"Excellent. Luke has kindly invited us to his family pub in town, where he had promised me food, drink, and plenty of alcohol. And best of all, no media allowed."

Charlie's expression was utter shock, and Andrea could see her friend try and find a way to back out of it before Luke tried to reassure her.

"Don't worry about the media, Charlie. They know better than to chance their arm with my da, and if they behave, I always pose for a picture or two. We will close to the general public, considering a few of my sister's band will probably rock up."

Well, that wasn't exactly what Andrea had in mind when she accepted Luke's offer for drinks. "Oh, you didn't say that the band might be there."

"That an issue?"

"Nope. No problem at all." Yeah, right...

Luke grinned, devilment in his eyes. "Excellent, and don't worry about the band, Andi, I'll keep ya dancing all night if you want." Luke winked, flirting with her. Andrea was totally down for spending a night dancing with the handsome F1 driver even if Charlie was giving her an amused look. And Andrea told Charlie her plans the moment Luke had left the room.

"I think you and Luke will make a fine dancing

pair but Andi, using him to make the rock god jealous is not going to work."

"Why the hell not?" Oh gossip...did Charlie know something she didn't about the guy all the media loved.

"Not my story to tell. But if you think hard about it, you'll figure it out."

Andrea played out every scenario in her mind until she was reminded of another handsome man who was keeping his true self hidden from the media and it was a damn shame.

"Well damn, that's a waste. But we could totally set him up with JJ."

"I already mentioned it days ago."

It was good to know her and Charlie were still on the same page.

They both chuckled and turned their attention to other topics, discussing Quinn's new race manager, some Rebel PR stuff, and then Charlie convinced Andi to come stay over at hers for the weekend before their plans turned to Christmas. Considering it was Charlie's first Christmas without her dad, Andrea wanted to make sure that her best friend wasn't alone so when Charlie suggested one of their causal Manchester dinners, Andrea was quick to agree.

"Sounds like a plan. My parents are heading to Spain and Rhys will be with his bandmates.... unless you want to see if he who shall not be named wants to spend Christmas with you?"

"Hell, no. Unless you want to get cosy with the rock god?" Charlotte shot back.

"I'd rather drink paint thinner." Andrea drawled then laughed.

They were still laughing when Luke showed up at the door again. "I forgot to mention, ladies, it's casual dress in the pub. We aren't that upmarket. Everyone is expected to arrive around nine so anything around then is grand." His phone rang, interrupting them, and gave a grumbled response before he hung up and said. "Ah, so that's sorted. Quinn is getting collected around nine by Noah so he is more than happy to pick you gals up. Just like one big happy family."

Luke slipped from the room as Andrea glanced at Charlie, saw the pained expression on her face before she offered Andrea a smile and told her to be at her house for drinks before this nightmare began to unfold. If Andrea hadn't been so worried about Charlie being in the same room with Noah, then she might have stressed herself out about being in the same room with the rock god and his ego...

There wasn't enough alcohol in Ireland to make this go smoothly...

CHAPTER SEVEN

HEARTACHE MELODY

Andrea

ANDREA HAD ARRIVED at Charlie's armed with enough beer and vodka to drink themselves into a stupor and found Charlie pacing the house in her underwear trying to decide what to wear. So, with two beers, Andrea nudged her upstairs and helped her pick out an outfit that made Charlie feel comfortable and less anxious.

When Charlie was suitably dressed in jeans and a blouse, her friend looked at Andrea's outfit and she teased. "The rock god will think you're a rock princess."

Andrea gave Charlie her trademark look that had made an intern or two cry. She hadn't made a conscious decision to dress up too much but a tiny part of her wanted to make Declan look twice at her and see what he had missed out on. Her skin-tight leather leggings clung to her lean legs and she wore a simple black vest that exposed her midriff. She had completed the rock-inspired look with a leather jacket gifted to her by JJ after she'd attended an award ceremony with him.

That man knew how to shop, bless him.

Andrea made sure that Charlie was laughing by the time Quinn knocked on the front door and Charlie made introductions. Quinn Murphy was petite and beautiful, her features marred by a seriousness and a darkness in her eyes that told Andrea that the girl racer had lived a hard life. Andrea could almost feel the tension rolling off the girl and knew there and then she had made the right choice with her new race manager Oskar. He would be a calm, steady presence by her side and something told Andrea that Quinn needed that.

They joked about keeping Noah waiting in the car, Quinn rolling her eyes as Charlie remarked. "Hell no! the last thing we need is a resurgence of moody, broody, teen Noah for keeping him waiting."

They downed their drinks, then headed out to see Mr. Broody in full glower, and his mood didn't improve as he received a call from his estranged mother. Andrea felt sorry for Noah as she heard the woman ask for more money and Noah basically told her to get lost and that he wasn't a cashpoint.

Andrea watched Charlie after Noah hung up and saw her friend try to make Noah feel better. She had not seen the two of them together, but watching the glint in Charlie's eyes when she teased Noah, Andrea could see just how much her friend still cared for him. When Charlie tugged on Noah's ear, teasing him about music, and then jerked back, Andrea could see the turmoil all over her face.

They arrived at Sullivan's bar, and Andrea and Quinn got out to give Charlie and Noah a few seconds of privacy. Andrea felt her heart begin to race as she pushed open the door to the pub and strode in, watching as Luna darted over to give Quinn a hug and it made Andrea smile to know that the girl had a friend in Luke's sister. It looked like Charlie's dad had made an excellent choice taking Quinn under his wing because it gave the young woman a circle of friends that Andrea herself had not known until she had met Charlie.

Declan lifted his blue eyes toward her and his frown deepened as he gaze raked over her and it immediately made Andrea feel like she was seventeen again and totally delusional for even thinking that Declan Walsh could be interested in lanky, unremarkable Andrea Collins.

The contact was broken when the band came up to her and welcomed her, asking her what she was drinking, and soon she was laughing, chatting back as if Declan was not trying to bore a hole in her with his stare.

Charlie came into the bar next and it was Rhys who spotted her first, her brother grinning from his seat as he yelled. "Charlie, darling, come sit on my lap!"

While Charlie laughed at Rhys, Andrea strode over, slapped her brother up side his head, Rhys not bothered in the slightest as he winked at Charlie He then introduced Charlie to Jameson Kent, Luna Sullivan, and last but not least, the rock god himself, Declan Walsh.

Andrea watched as Charlie gave him a warm smile as her best friend assessed the man who had caused Andrea all her heartache. Declan curved his lips into a smile that threatened to suck the air from Andrea's lungs before she remembered that Declan hated her, his glare as he excused himself to go over to where Noah was sitting at the bar punctuating that point.

Glancing away, Andrea saw the heated exchange between Noah and Charlie, knew that whatever was between them was as electrifying as ever but Andrea wanted to help her friend. She nudged Charlie's shoulder, dragging her gaze away from Noah as Andrea announced. "I'm gasping!"

When Andrea forgot that she was in the same room as Declan, which was fucking hard to do, she felt an easy kinship with the other members of the band, enjoyed flirting with Luke and Jameson and even more so when Charlie did, earning her a darkened look from Noah.

Andrea sipped on her bottle of beer as she chatted to Luna about getting her some interviews just for her because having a female drummer who could actually drum just as well as, if not better than some of the men in bands made Luke's twin beam. She rambled on for ages about trying to get the boys to do more social media stuff and Andrea promised to help her drag them into the new age instead of the stone age.

They drank and danced, Charlie's carefree laugh warming Andrea's bones as Noah continued to glance in her friend's direction when he thought no one was watching, and Andrea waited until Declan punched Noah in the arm with a grin, then Declan walked between Jameson and Andrea as they danced, pushing his bandmate so that he went off balance, Jameson just laughing.

Then Andrea took her chance and strode toward Noah Donovan as he nursed his drink at the bar. "I think we may have gotten off on the wrong foot."

Noah quirked his brow, shifting in his seat so he faced her, and Andrea perched herself on the seat Declan had vacated and blocked Charlie from view.

"We may never be besties," she began, tapping he fingers on her thigh. "But we should clear the air for Charlie's sake. I know you are important to her, so we have to get along."

"I'm not important to Charlie anymore." Noah

snorted before calling for another drink and Andrea gave Noah her best ballbusting look

"If you think that, then you really are a fucking dumbass." Andrea shot back at him, rolling her eyes. "Charlie has this big heart. Once she lets you in there, she doesn't let you out. She would murder me for saying it, but we never missed a race. We never not celebrated a win for the team, for you. Whatever reason you two fell out, now's your chance to make amends. Fuck it up, Noah, and she will be snapped up by someone who deserves that heart of hers."

The race car driver looked shocked that Andrea was being so brutally honest with him and she could see the moment Noah began to respect her. "Why help me? Why tell me all this?"

"Because when two people look at each other like you two do, it can only end in love or hate. And I don't think Charlie has hate in her."

That made Noah sit up ramrod straight before he offered her his own advice as he glanced over her shoulder to where Declan was no doubt watching the exchange. "Maybe you should take your own advice, Andi."

Andrea let loose a bark of laughter, felt eyes on her as she shook her head. "I don't do romance. And I don't date musicians. So, sort your own shit out and I'll worry about mine."

She slipped off the barstool, her mission complete even if Charlie might not appreciate her meddling but

Andrea had a knack for reading people and it was totally obvious to anyone that Charlie and Noah had a lot of residual feelings and things that needed to be resolved. She might not be able to come to terms with her car crash of a romantic life but she could help her Charlie.

She meant what she said when she told Noah she didn't do romance. She'd had a few one-night stands, even dated a footballer for a while, but she never had the connection like Charlie and Noah had, unless you count the one she thought she'd had with Declan.

Andrea chastised herself for heading down that road again, called for the music be turned up, earning a whoop from everyone but Noah and Declan, as a familiar song came on and Andrea forced Charlie to dance with her a little more.

CHAPTER EIGHT

Andrea

IT DIDN'T TAKE LONG for the night to get out of hand but when you had rockstars and adrenaline junkies in the same room, it was bound to get a little rowdy. Both Luke and Rhys were close to being hammered when some old-school dance track came on the speakers. Luke decided it would be funny to get up on a chair and dance like no one was watching, throwing his hands up in the air.

Luke wobbled where he stood, and Quinn reached out to steady him, before Luke slumped down onto the seat and called for more shots, Andrea smiling as his dad ignored the request and instead turned down the music.

But her brother was far from ready to start winding down the party and reached over the bar and pulled out a bottle of tequila with a lopsided grin. Andrea saw Noah get ready to get up off his seat, ready to intervene if he needed to and he might have to because Rhys and Luke were downing the tequila like it was nothing.

Noah slid off his seat and stalked towards the two drunk idiots but Andrea was worried about how much Rhys was drinking. Rhys had always used alcohol as a means to cope with his dyslexia, especially when they were younger and he liked to party. Noah's face looked murderous as he came toward them but it was Charlie who decided to be the one to calm things down.

"Okay Rhys, that's enough tequila for Luke. I'm sure he doesn't want me to pull rank and tell him that he has an afternoon training session that will be a bitch with a hangover."

Luke groaned, running his hands through his tousled hair. "Ugh, boss is right. No more tequila for Luke."

Rhys shrugged like it didn't bother him that his drinking buddy was being ridiculously sensible all of a sudden and took a slug from the bottle. Declan reached over from where he was sitting. Grabbing the bottle, he handed it off to Noah with a fluidness that gave Andrea the impression that this wasn't the first time Declan had been forced to take a bottle from her brother. Andrea watched in shock as a dark look crept over Rhys's face for a microsecond before it vanished and her brother was smiling like it was no big deal.

The music dulled to a low murmur. Noah inclined his head to Declan, who pointed to the seat beside him and Noah sat down. Charlie looked a little pale as she went to the bar, and Andrea was about to check on her when Quinn approached Charlie, then Quinn shouted her farewells. Noah went over to Quinn and Andrea plonked down on a stool and gave her aching feet a rest, ignoring a certain rockstar.

"You okay?"

Andrea was startled to hear Declan ask her the question that she didn't know what to say when she turned and he was sitting right there across from her. Her mouth felt dry and she took a sip of her beer, Declan's eyes not leaving hers before she replied. "I'm good thanks."

She hadn't meant her tone to sound frosty and it made Declan frown, scratching at his beard as he sighed. "You think we can just be civil with each other so we don't make it awkward for everyone else. I've had Rhys bending my ear all day asking if you being our manager is going to be an issue and Luna telling me to be nicer to you."

"I was perfectly fine ignoring you so that this unpleasantness didn't spoil the evening. You are the one who just sat down and immediately started having a go."

A muscle ticked in Declan's jaw, then he switched

gears. "You went to the fire station to see Eric yesterday."

That made Andrea smile without any effort. She had been passing the fire station yesterday and decided to stop in and see if Eric was on duty. The youngest of the Walsh triplets had scooped her up into his arms the moment she walked into the fire station and ordered her round to his mam's for dinner some night.

The cheeky git also promised to make sure his oldest brother knew he wasn't invited.

"I was passing by. Who would have thought that the baby who had stayed in the nicu the longest would be running into burning buildings? He's still as cheeky as I remember."

"He told me he asked you out."

It was a statement said in the harshest of tones that plucked at the strings of her temper as she rolled her eyes. The triplets were a few years younger than her and Declan and despite the fact that all of the Walsh men were handsome and mostly charming, Andrea had no interest in the younger men. For fuck sake, she used to babysit them. Was Declan actually getting all bent out of shape because he thought she would go out with his little brother?

Ugh....Declan Walsh was not

"Your brother asked me out and I told him he was wasting his time flirting with me since I remember him having to go to accident and emergency when he decided to jump off your roof and bounced right off your neighbour's trampoline and broke his arm."

Andrea knew her tone had turned vicious, but Declan seemed to drag that reaction from her. She leaned in closer to Declan, saw his nostrils flare. "I also told your brother that I had changed since I last saw him and didn't waste my time with boys when I spend my time with drop-dead gorgeous men who know how to treat a woman. I don't plan on scratching an itch with any men from Cork."

A growl rumbled in Declan's throat but Andrea cut across him as he made to speak. "Don't. you don't get to be an asshole to me for years and then act like a possessive ex. Who I chose to sleep with doesn't concern you and never will. So, take your let's be civil and shove it up your ass, Declan."

Andrea pulled back as Charlie sat down beside her, taking her drink and downing it after her own encounter with Noah. Declan had taken out his acoustic guitar and was quietly strumming it.

Luke and Luna's dad told them he wanted to shut up the bar, looking tired and Luna told him to head off and they would clean up. Luke's dad left with a warning not to wreck the place. Andrea was tapping her fingers along to the chords Declan was playing when he lifted his eyes to look at her best friend.

"You sing?" he asked Charlie, and Andrea hared that she felt jealous that he would ask Charlie and not her. Then her friend laughed and she felt super guilty for feeling jealous where Charlie was concerned.

"Hell no," Charlotte laughed, then nudged Andi's shoulder. "But Andi does."

It felt like being cut open and she was seventeen again, playing the piano and Declan telling her that it was a pity she couldn't sing because they could use her in the band. She had been so self-conscious that she couldn't sing in front of him, had begged Rhys to not tell Declan and he had agreed because he hadn't wanted to make his sister uncomfortable.

And now, now Declan would know and her stomach felt sick.

Declan's eyes slowly shifted from Charlotte to Andi, then he smirked and it dissipated her nerves and sparked her fury as he said "Andi doesn't sing."

"Not for you anyway." She bit back; her words full of venom.

Charlie was grinning wide as she held out her hand for the guitar, taking it from Declan before she handed it to Andrea and the guitar felt familiar in her hands, not the first time she had played this guitar.

Rhys slapped Declan on the shoulder. "You're about to get schooled, mate. Andi had a record deal long before us. Then they wanted her to go into a girl band and she walked."

Declan looked shocked as he barked at her. "How the hell did I not know this? Rhys didn't tell me."

"You never asked. Plus, it's none of your business."

Andi swept her hair off her face, giving herself a minute before she told herself that this was just like the many times that she had sung in the student bar she worked on open mic nights and not at all daunting that she was singing in front the man with a voice like whiskey.

She ignored the rapid beating of her heart, let herself have faith in the music and the way the guitar felt under her fingers as the gathered crowd went silent as she started to play the first few chords of The Parting Glass. As she fell into the music, Andrea closed her eyes, took a deep breath, and opened her mouth to sing.

CHAPTER NINE

Declan

CARESSED him like she was singing just for him and him alone. Declan had a quote written on the wall in his studio that read: *"Music shouldn't be just a tune, it should be a touch."*

And that's what Andi was doing, her husky tone like fingers grazing his skin, and damn he was awestruck. He remembered the first time he had gone to see a band live, felt the spike of a adrenaline as the crowd cheered, the lights went down and there was this hush of silence before the music started and the band began their set, and Declan was addicted.

Now, Andi was centre stage, stealing the limelight and he was one hundred percent behind it.

How had he never known? How had she kept this big a secret from him on nights they had written lyrics together, sorted out melodies, and when Andi hummed along, never singing the words, he should have known that Andi could sing even better than he could.

Declan was aware that Charlie was watching him watch Andi, as she concluded the final bars of the song, her fingers gracefully plucking at the strings of the guitar. Then Andi opened her eyes, and Declan still hadn't managed to take a breath as everyone clapped and cheered for Andi.

Handing Declan back his guitar, Andi didn't even bother to look at him as she muttered what he thought was thanks before she looked at Charlie. But Charlie was distracted by the fact that Noah had gotten to his feet and stormed out, the door to the bar banging shut as his friend made a noisy exit.

Rhys had fallen asleep in the corner of the room and Jameson was dragging him to his feet and told Declan he would make sure he got home okay. Luna went to fix Luke a coffee so her brother could help her tidy up.

Declan wasn't able to take his eyes off of Andi, realized he was frowning at her as Charlie turned and asked Andi if she was ready to leave. Before he knew it, the girls were heading toward the door and he couldn't just leave her walk away after that.

"Andi, wait."

Andi froze at the sound of his voice, nodding her head when Charlie asked her if she would be okay. Andi inclined her head and Declan followed out after her as Andi shivered in the cold night air and all he wanted to do was take her in his arms and warm her up.

"What do you want, Declan? It's cold and my feet hurt."

Declan ran his hands through his hair. "Why did you never tell me you could sing?"

Andi shrugged and Declan saw a sliver of the Andi he had fallen for as a teenager, the hesitance and lack of confidence. "I couldn't sing in front of you back then. Every time I tried, my throat just closed up and I panicked."

"You didn't have to be nervous with me, Andi."

Andi frowned and shook her head. "You don't understand."

Declan folded his arms across his chest. "Then tell me so I understand. We used to tell each other everything. What changed, Andi?"

Rubbing her arms absently, Andi looked uncomfortable as she mumbled. "It doesn't matter now. It really doesn't matter."

"It fucking matters to me, Andi. How did we get here to where you can't stand to look at me or stand to be in the same room as me without looking like I'm the antichrist?" He asked, no demanded from Andi.

Maybe it was his tone, maybe it was the demand in

it but it snapped something in Andi. "You happened. I had my entire life planned out and you went and tossed a grenade on my life. Did you use me to boost your ego, Dec? Was it fun to have me trail after you like a puppy when you didn't feel anything for me? Did you all have a good laugh at my expense?"

Where the hell was this all coming from? How could Andi think that he would use her like that? Surely he couldn't have imagined the electricity between them when their fingers brushed against one another's when passing instruments or drinks to one another. Surely he had seen the same need in her eyes as he had in his own when their eyes clashed.

"I have no clue what you are talking about, Andi?"

Andi threw her hands up in the air. "That's the point, Declan...You have no clue what you've done because it wasn't a big deal to you. Rhys might have been your best friend, but you were mine! But then you just... and I ... And I ...I ..."

Clamping her mouth shut, like she hadn't intended to say all she had and then Andi shook her head, her loose caramel curls bouncing with the movement. Dread filled his stomach as he looked at her face, the sadness in her eyes as if he was the root cause of it all.

But she was the one who had left him standing alone in the rain like a lemon. She was the one who ghosted him and then left the goddamn country without offering any explanation and now she was standing there with those big eyes of hers, acting like the injured party.

"You stood me up, remember?" He snarled, the hurt feelings resurfacing. "You left me waiting for you to come and you never showed. You wouldn't even speak to me and I never knew why. I called you a million times wanting to know what I did wrong and you just took off to another country and forgot about me. What did I do that was so wrong? Why the fuck did you ghost me?"

Then Andi laughed, incensing him even more as he took a step toward her.

"Don't you fucking laugh at me, Andi. Don't."

"Or what?" she tossed back at him, but she glanced at the door as if she was scared of him and he couldn't blame her. "You'll make my life hell? You'll shun me so no one talks to me anymore You'll date a girl I hated just to get back at me? Do your worst, Declan. Do your worst because you already broke my heart once and I'll be damned if I'll let you do it again. Go fuck yourself."

"Is everything okay here?"

Declan whirled round to see Charlie standing there looking at them with a worried expression and Declan realized they must have been shouting. He held up his hands in a way of apology as a car pulled into the car park and Andi shook her head, her eyes watery, and jumped into the back of the car, slamming the door shut.

"Are you okay?"

Declan laughed at the softness in Charlie's tone. "I'm grand, Charlie. Go and make sure that Andi's okay. She seemed upset."

Charlie regarded him for a moment as if she was assessing him. She chewed on her bottom lip and then sighed. "She would kill me for interfering, but I think you're a good man, Declan. It's not my place to say but you hurt her, back then. And you continued to hurt her when she was already down. That's why she bolted. She had a valid reason and I think it pains her that you can't even remember what you said or did to kill whatever was happening between you. Because she certainly never forgot."

Charlie rested a hand on his arm. "We never forget the ones who obliterated our hearts no matter how badass we get."

The window on the car rolled down and Andi shouted for Charlie to hurry up and Charlie rolled her eyes as she headed toward the car, glancing over her shoulder with a rue smile before she got in and the car was gone a few seconds later.

Declan stood out in the frigid air and replayed what had just happened over in his mind but he was left with nothing. Up until he had been stood up, he had thought things between him and Andi were fine. Only a day before, he had almost kissed her, had almost given in to the urge he'd been fighting for months and he had decided that the night of the concert, he was going to confess all to Andi, even if it meant he and Rhys fell out.

"I think it pains her that you can't even remember what you said or did to kill whatever was happening between you. Because she certainly never forgot."

Hearing Charlie say the words, seeing the hurt on Andi's face...it made him determined to find out exactly what had been the catalyst that had caused the rift between them. He could be a stubborn SOB when he wanted to and Andi was going to reveal all to him, whether she liked it or not.

CHAPTER TEN

Declan

A FEW DAYS had passed since he and Andi had stood outside Sullivans and argued, and Declan had been in a pissed off mood since then. It had annoyed him even more than Andi was ignoring his voicenotes about deadlines and possible gigs coming up. She listened to them but never replied. Andi was ghosting him ...again.

Even Rhys had kept his mouth shut where his sister was concerned, just telling Declan that Andi had gone back to Manchester and planned to stay there over Christmas with Charlie. Declan knew why Charlie had made a sudden departure across the water, considering Noah told him he had finally come clean about what happened when they were younger and Charlie had run from the truth.

To be honest, Declan had spent the last few days thinking about the past, trying to put the pieces together to see if he could pinpoint the moment, any event that blew up his relationship with Andi, and for the life of him, he couldn't.

Of course, he knew dating Lauren would annoy Andi, that's why he hooked up with her that night at her party. A stupid, childish reaction that he had guilt about to this day. He had been so pissed off that all he'd wanted to do was hurt Andi, and he'd succeeded.

No wonder she hated him, but she had ghosted him before that and that was bugging the hell out of him.

Declan closed his eyes, hearing the erotic sound of Andi singing in his head as he drowned himself in memories of her, before everything went to hell.

The clock struck two in the morning in unison with the rapturous sounds of Rhys snoring from his bed as Declan rolled over and looked up at the ceiling. He had been finding it increasingly hard to fall asleep in the Collins' house lately, knowing that Andi was lying in her bed next door.

He didn't know the exact moment his feelings for Andi had changed, it had been a gradual thing, slow and steady until it became all-consuming, like an addiction. He noticed more how her eyes lit up when she found new music or the way she tucked her hair behind her ears and chewed on her bottom lip when she was concentrating hard.

He'd started calling even when he knew Rhys was busy, just to spend time with her, spending hours traipsing through record stores and music shops and playing the instruments that they dreamed of having enough money to buy.

There came a creak on the floorboards outside of Rhys's bedroom, and Declan darted upright, knowing the sound of Andi's footfalls as well as the way his heart beat. He listened as she went down the stairs, then he was pulling on his tee and out of the bed, following after her, careful to avoid the obvious creaks on the stairs.

Declan searched the entire house for Andi, before realizing that she would have slipped out to the family music room, its soundproofed walls the perfect tranquil place for her to practice. Her dad had built the outside shed, a builder by trade and it was where he and the Collins' siblings spent a lot of time.

He stepped out into the garden, shivering at the cold until he heard Andi at the keyboard playing the first few keys of Bring me the Horizon's, Can you feel my heart? It was one of Andi's favourite bands and songs, and Declan knew all of Andi's favourite songs off by heart.

He knew that she loved David Gray's This Years Love and cried every time she watched reruns of Dawson's Creek and Joey finally realized she was meant to be with Pacey. He knew she considered Maniac 2000 by Mark McCabe to be the best dance song of all time and Linkin Park's, in the End, one of the best songs ever recorded. She pretended she didn't know all the lyrics to Bewitched, C'est le Vie because she was too cool for that.

She wore band tees and jeans, but only if she really liked a band. She loved to find music from a band that no one had discovered yet and see them in the smallest of venues rather than arena tours because the acoustics were better. She wanted to go to Reading & Leeds or Download Festival instead of electric picnic. She knew a song was good, no matter the genre if it invoked an emotion from someone. She didn't believe like autotuned songs and preferred someone who dared to sing off tune then let a computer alter their voice.

Declan stood outside the music room in the freezing cold and tried to summon the courage to walk inside and tell Andi that he saw her, all of her. But he was afraid that she wouldn't feel the same or worse she would see that he wasn't good enough for her. She deserved to soar and he would try and keep her here, with him and that wouldn't be fair.

So he listened outside until his fingers and toes got numb before Declan retreated back into the house and under the warmth of the covers. He lingered, awake until she came back up the stairs, pausing outside the bedroom door for what felt like an age before she sighed and went back into her own room and closed the door behind her.

"Earth to Deco..."

Declan had forgotten that he was sat in the studio

with Jameson, trying to write some songs for their debut album. Jameson Kent had been his next-door neighbour for years but it was music that had brought them together, much like it had with Rhys. Jamie could sing but preferred to play guitar and not let anyone know he wrote many of the lyrics.

Jamie was pretty reserved for the most part, and had a heart-breaking story where his girlfriend had died in a hit and run when they were sixteen. Layla had pushed Jameson out of the way and she had died in his arms as the driver sped off, high as a kite when he was arrested hours later asleep in the car.

Layla had also been his sister's friend, but he and Niamh were as close as Rhys and Andi were, hadn't minded it when they got together. Jameson went off the rails for a few years after, trying to deal with everything but Declan and Rhys had been there to remind him that Layla wouldn't want him to ruin his life when she had sacrificed herself for him.

Jameson had even written a song about Layla that Declan was trying to persuade him to put on the album, even if it was Declan that sung it, but he was trying hard to get Jamie to be the one who put his grief and his pain in the song.

"I'm sorry, Jay." Declan sighed as he dragged his fingers through his hair. "My mind's not in this today."

Jameson gave him a sly grin. "I can understand. Andi, man...she's a knockout."

Jealousy surged through him and he lifted his eyes

to the grinning Jamie, who just chuckled and slapped his hand on his knew. "Deco, your face man. You look ready to murder me. I have no designs on Andi, but I can totally admire that she looks hella good, even more so after hearing that voice. She was incredible. You need to fix whatever dickheadery you did to fuck that up, Dec."

Declan snorted. "You assume it's me that fucked up?"

Jameson's arched brow told Declan he wasn't believing any other explanation.

"I watched the two of you at the bar. Mate, if this was a romance novel, all those angry lustful looks would make for the hottest sex ever."

Declan barked out a laugh and rolled his eyes as Jamie grinned. "You've been spending too much time working in your sister's bookshop."

His sister owned a quaint bookshop in the city centre called Rebel Books and Jameson helped out as much as he could, hell even Declan had gotten behind the counter during last Christmas when the shop had been super busy.

"What can I say," Jamie shrugged his broad shoulders. "Chicks love a dude who can read *and* is in a band."

"I'm pretty sure girls who read a lot of books don't like to be referred to as chicks."

Jamie waved him off as he strummed his guitar and tapped a hand on the body of the guitar.

"Niamh still dating dickhead Brian?"

"Yup." That was all that Jamie said in response, but Declan knew Jameson didn't like his sister's boyfriend one bit, or how much he was trying to change Niamh.

Was that what had happened with Andi? Had he done something like that to make Andi run from him, to hate him?

"Dec?" Jameson broke through his thoughts again and Declan lifted his gaze to look into the pained expression of one of his closest friends. "If Andi is the one you can't get out of your head, then go and tell her. Life is too fucking short to keep that shit to yourself. I never got the chance to tell Layla that I loved her. But you can do that, with Andi. Don't waste any more time pretending she's not it for ya, man. Go get your girl."

CHAPTER ELEVEN

Andrea

ANDREA AND CHARLIE had spent their entire Christmas holed up in their apartment or working in Rebel PR in order to keep their minds off their hometown drama. For once, it was Andrea who had to play good cop when Charlie ripped Nicolette a new one for interfering in Rebel Racers business when she was entrusted not to. It was one of the few times, Andrea had heard Charlie raise her voice and when Charlie asked Nicolette if she wanted to be sacked, their former classmate burst into tears.

It had taken that emotional outburst for Charlie to spill the beans to Andrea and tell her all about Noah and her dad and all that shady mess and Andrea had just let Charlie cry on her shoulder and fed her ice cream and alcohol, hanging up on all the calls Noah had been blowing up her phone with.

They had a sombre Christmas, just the two of them on the couch stuffing their faces with selection boxes and watching movies. JJ had even stopped by to spend Stephen's day with them, offering to take them to some tropical resort to unwind but they declined because they still had work to do even if they were running on chocolate and carbs.

Charlie was still in contact with the factory back home getting stuff sorted for testing and signing all the paperwork before they all travelled and Andrea was in constant contact with the record company, going over the finer points and agreeing to some deadlines while networking to get some air time and interviews for the band.

Andrea herself was also doing a stellar job of ignoring all the damn voicenotes Declan was sending her. Listening to his voice all the time was like a kick to the stomach but she kept on listening to them because she was a goddamn idiot.

Hey Andi, it's me...it's Declan...look...umm...oh for fuck sake...can you stop ignoring my calls and texts and just me...stop ignoring me...we need to talk and you blanking me isn't working. I can't concentrate with all this hanging over us...just talk to me Andi... Come on, please.

The please had almost broken her resolve and she had lingered with her hand over the call button before she tossed the phone aside, trying to stop his pained tone from playing over and over in her mind. She wanted to focus on getting things in place and helping Charlie get her head straight before she had to get on her flight in a few weeks for testing.

On one of the nights after Christmas, when Charlie was up to her eyes in work, Andrea had agreed to go for dinner with JJ so Charlie could have some peace. And she loved Joshua James like another brother and was happy to be wined and dined for an evening if he meant she just got to be in his company.

Now she sat across from JJ in the ridiculously expensive and hard-to-get-a-table restaurant, the envy of many a woman and man in the room as JJ smiled at her with his Hollywood smile and charm.

She sipped on her wine, wishing it was a nice cold beer and laughed when JJ reached over and took her glass, sliding his own bottle of beer over for her to drink.

"You can't take me anywhere," Andrea said laughing as JJ just continued to smile.

"I would ask the waiter to bring us a pitcher of beer if only to see your gorgeous smile. My two favourite ladies have been rather subdued the last few weeks."

Andrea flashed him a sad smile before taking a sip of her beer. She had told JJ a little of what went on, if only to get a man's perspective but Charlie needed to vent because she and adored her father and since he

was now deceased, there was no way for her to have it
out with him and get it off her chest and she was struggling to cope with that.

Her little drama with Declan paled in
comparison.

"You have that adorable scrunchy face you get
when you are thinking too hard, darling."

Andrea rolled her eyes at JJ, who leaned across the
table and took her hand in his, the flash of camera's
going off a thing Andrea had gotten used to when she
hung out with JJ, it didn't really bother her that much
anymore.

But she wondered what Declan would think when
he saw the pictures, of her all glammed up and sitting
across the way from JJ, him holding her hand. Would
he be jealous or would he think even less of her than he
already did?

"Don't make yourself sound cheap, Andi."

That's exactly what he had said when Andrea had
told him that she enjoyed being in JJ's company and
they were just friends. She liked walking red carpets
and just being with a male friend where there was no
pretence or expectations.

"Jesus Andi, you're in love with this Declan."

Of course, JJ would see through and get to the
bones of it. But she was still gonna try and deny it.

"I was...I might still ..." Andrea huffed out a breath
as she patted JJ's knuckles with the hand he wasn't
holding. "I think I might be as bad as Charlie. I'm

holding onto feelings for a boy who didn't even like me...how sad am I?"

"It's not sad, darling. He hurt you but you still remember the good times. If your Declan was pretending the whole time then I surely have competition for an Oscar."

Maybe JJ was right...maybe she should hear Declan out and finally put the ghosts of their past behind them. It would make it easier on the band, hell even Rhys would feel better if the two most important people in his life were not at loggerheads all the time.

She could be friends with Declan, right?

Shaking her head to clear her thoughts, Andrea lifted JJ's hand to her mouth and pressed a kiss to the back if his hand. The actor quirked his brows in amusement as the cameras went wild again.

"Ugh," Andrea said with an exaggerated sigh, letting a smile curl up her lips. "Why is life so unfair? Why did the universe send you to me and then just mock me by making you love penis? Life is so cruel!"

JJ barked out a laugh so loud that the diners who had not been watching them were now staring at them. Water leaked from JJ's eyes and that made Andrea laugh so hard until the waiter arrived with their mains and gave them a look of disdain that had them both laughing again.

Andrea was happy when the conversation veered to JJ asking Andrea her advice on a few roles he was in contention for, and JJ listened to Andrea, taking on board her advice like he had done a few times. He valued her opinion and that meant a lot to Andrea.

At the end of the night, JJ drove her back to her apartment, standing on the footpath outside and running his hands up and down her arms when she shivered. Andrea was aware of the paparazzi lurking nearby and she smiled when JJ bent down to kiss her cheek and thanked her for a pleasant evening.

Andrea rolled her eyes, nudged his shoulder, and told him to give her a shout next week and let her know if he decided to take the roles they talked about. She walked away, feeling happier than she had since she walked into the penthouse and realized it was Heartache Melody she was to manage but then she heard JJ call her name.

He came forward, embracing her in a hug as he leaned in to whisper in her ear. "Love isn't rational. You can fall in love with the wrong person and it could still be love. The world can be a dark and twisted place but love can get you through it. You let your guard down and he hurt you. but he doesn't know how you feel, darling. How you felt. He needs to know why and how he hurt you. would you not want to know if it was the other way around?"

JJ stepped away and winked, striding away to his car, glancing over his shoulder.

"Love ya, JJ!" she yelled, laughing as he blew her a kiss, shouting that he loved her too before he ducked into his car and the engine roared to life.

JJ, the soppy git, was right...she needed to get things off her chest and she would do it when she went back to Cork. She decided to throw Declan and bone, texting him and telling him she would be in Cork in a few weeks and they should sit down and chat.

On her way to her apartment, Andrea watched as the message went from sent to read, saw the bubbles that indicated that Declan was responding, her heart in her mouth until the bubbles stopped and then nothing....

Looked like Declan was giving her a taste of her own medicine.

CHAPTER TWELVE

Andrea

"WHAT CAN I GETCHA?"

Andrea grinned as she took the order for drinks and pulled a pint in the busy bar, delighted that she had managed to persuade Charlie to come out and join her. When her old boss texted her after seeing that she was in town after her night out with JJ, he had demanded Andrea come and sing at the Uni's popular open mic night.

She'd texted a few of the old college crew and told them her and Charlie would be going to "The Basement", the nickname of the bar that was literally in the basement of the student centre. It was a cramped, small room with a stage and a smattering of tables but Andrea had loved working here throughout her course and even though they had long since graduated, there was nothing like coming back.

Hell, even Charlie had gotten into the spirit of it, collecting glasses and she even looked happy chatting with the old crew. Her old boss had decided that this would be an oldies night and banished any college-aged kid from the room the moment they had all poured into the basement.

The music was cranked up and soon Andrea was swept away in the familiarness and the camaraderie. She tended bar and danced and laughed when open mic night turned into really bad karaoke as the lads got stuck in and butchered a few tunes. It was easy to forget that Declan hadn't answered her, that his calls had ceased and any communication with the band was done through other members of the band.

And she would be lying to herself if she hadn't checked her phone a dozen times over the last few days, her heart racing every time her phone chimed. For a few days she had obsessively checked her brother's social media, for the chance to spot what the band was up to but even Rhys had been very quiet online.

The only inclination that the band were doing anything productive was when Luna shared a video of her, dressed in just her bra and shorts, her blood-red hair pulled back off her face as she absolutely killed it performing Foo Fighter's *The Pretender*. When she finished she swung the camera around to give the audience a quick view of the rest of the band clapping.

All expect Declan...

Andi strode past a few of their friends gathered round as the lads tried to out car Charlie, offering up advice and suggestion for her when it comes to cars and livery and all that stuff. Charlie was giving as good as she got, telling them all about the fact that she was the one who had told her dad to have the cars in Irish green and cork red, betting the lads that she could get behind the wheel of any of their cars and win them in a race.

Andrea knew that Charlie needed the break, to just be surrounded with people who were not intimidated because she was now Charlotte Coyle, CEO of Rebel Racers and owner of Rebel PR, but remembered her as Charlie, who once built a soapbox car out of cardboard and old wheels and raced around the quad for charity. Who was not averse to childish drinking games, or a game of truth and dare.

Charlie had spent the night laughing and joking, smiling and she just seemed lighter than she had over the last couple of weeks. It had taken a lot of begging and pleading to get her here tonight and now, as she glanced at Charlie as she mock punched Shane in the arm, Andrea was glad they had come.

Shane Carter was a close friend of theirs from college, another Cork lad who had transferred to their course in the second year and of course, all the Irish kids stuck together. Both herself and Charlie were hoping to persuade Shane to come back and take up a position in their Cork office, managing the sports side of the business, considering Andi was an idiot when it came to sports and Charlie would have her hands full with Rebel Racers.

As if he sensed her watching him, Shane looked up and flashed her a dazzling smile. "Collins! Get your fine ass up and give us a tune."

Andrea laughed as everyone started chanting her name and she rolled her eyes. She slid the glasses she had collected along the bar, smacking Shane at the back of the head like she would Rhys, and made her way up on the stage to the beat-up old piano.

It had been ages since she'd played it, so she gave herself a few practice tries before she got down and truly belted out a track. She started by playing Darude *Sandstorm*, then Robert Miles, *Children*, then a little bit of Eiffel 65 with *Blue* that had everyone cheering. She slowed down the tempo to follow up with a little barber's adagio for strings. She finished off her 90's mix with a nod to one of Manchester's own bands and played *Wonderwall* by Oasis.

When she finished, she ignored the cheers and the calls for one more tune and tapped the microphone to make sure if it was working before she held up her hand for the gang of misfits to simmer down before she took a deep breath, closed her eyes and started singing Dermot Kennedy's Rome. Andrea loved the song, admittedly because it reminded her of Declan, the old Declan, who stayed up late to discuss lyrics and music.

All the pain of the last few weeks, Andrea poured it into the song, as if the music could wash away some of the hurt and anger. Her fingers danced on the keys effortlessly and Andrea knew that she should find more time to just be her, to do more of what she liked, what gave her a sense of peace.

Andrea finished up the song, opening her eyes and inclining her head as everyone clapped and cheered. Shane got up and put a pint on the piano, grinning as Andrea took more than a gulp from it before she spoke into the microphone.

"All right, ya bloody heathens, simmer down now." That earned her another chortle of laughter. "It's been good to be back here, in our second home, even if you all are a bunch of misfits."

There was a good-humoured banter tossed back about blow-ins and foreigners that Andrea and Charlie were well used to, but when Andrea whistled, they all hushed down, well used to Andrea giving orders.

"We've had a shite few weeks, me and our newest boss bitch, who by the way is kicking ass and taking names and teaching all the boys that it's girls who run the world." Charlie lifted her pint with a grin and Andrea continued. "But after tonight, with you lot, it's all grand and we can go back to conquering the world, one industry at a time."

Andrea hesitated before she continued. "Going back where you grew up, seeing old friends and family, makes you nostalgic and stirs up old feelings...old memories. So, here is a song that reminds me of home, of the past, and all that jazz."

Closing her eyes again, Andrea blew out a breath before she let her fingers glide over the piano, the melody of Adele's *Hometown* echoing in the extremely acoustic bar and she played until the song called for her to sing and Andrea sang, her mind wandering to weeks ago, when she had first arrived back in Cork and had just wandered around the city centre, music in her ears as she took in the subtle changes that had happened since she had been gone and how good it felt to be back where some of her best memories were...and some of her worst.

When Andrea finished, she gave herself a couple of seconds before she opened her eyes and turned to grin at her friends to see if they wanted another song. But the bar had gone deathly silent and she wondered what had happened in other to suddenly shut all of the loudmouths up.

She glanced at Charlie, who just looked over her shoulder and back, and Andrea, her eyes widening as she mouthed, Oh my god....

Andrea narrowed her gaze and looked in the direction that everyone was now staring at the stairs that led down into the bar. She wasn't sure that a heart could survive the absolute shock that absorbed her, as well as everyone else in the bar.

This was not happening. She closed her eyes, thinking she had somehow conjured him here just by thinking about him, singing as if he could hear her and sure as if the universe was looking to mess with her head and especially mess with her heart.

The reason why Declan Walsh was not in any of the band's posts or videos was because he was here, in Manchester, standing at the bottom of the basement stairs with his stupid handsome face and Andrea forgot how to breathe.

CHAPTER THIRTEEN

Andrea

ANDREA ROSE off the seat at the piano with legs that felt like jelly. Everyone in the bar was looking from her to the new face of Irish rock who stood brooding at the bottom of the steps, his eyes focused on Andrea and no one else. Someone said her name and it snapped her out of her shocked state and spurred her into action.

She descended the steps leading up to the stage and made to cross the room when Charlie blocked her way. "I can tell him go, if you want. Or I can check into a hotel so you two can *talk*."

Andrea rolled her eyes at the implication in Charlie's tone as she muttered. "Not if he was the last man on earth, Charlie. I'll get rid of him."

Blocking out the hushed murmurs from her friends, Andrea strode right up to Declan, ignoring the depth of his blue eyes as she folded her arms across her chest, Declan's gaze dipping to her breasts before his lips tilted upwards.

"I feel like an idiot for never knowing that you had a voice like that."

Declan's tone was husky, heated, his eyes even more so but Andrea had nerves of steel, or at least she did with everyone but the too damn gorgeous man standing with his eyes focused on her. His hair was mused in that I just got out of bed look and his beard was thick and framed his full lips like a caress.

"You are a goddamn idiot for rocking up here for no reason!"

His grin deepened, that look of devilment in his eyes that no doubt made many a groupie drop their knickers for him in an instant. Hell, the way he was looking at her now, Andrea was tempted to drag him back to her place and give her body what it wanted, what it craved.

"You said you wanted to talk and I was in the neighbourhood."

"Cut the bullshit, Declan. What the hell are you doing here?"

Declan glanced around, then shrugged. "This is a bar, right? I think I fancy a pint."

"You are not stopping for a pint!" she hissed but Declan was already making his way to the bar, her fucking traitorous friends all stopping to say hello to the rockstar as if they didn't deal with famous people on a daily basis. Declan grinned as he took pictures and was the epitome of a global rock star before Andrea stormed behind the bar and poured him a pint.

When Declan finally managed to make his way through his newfound fans, he downed his pint like it was water and then leaned on the bar, folding his arms across the bar. His gaze dipped down and he smirked. "Nice t-shirt."

It was only then that Andrea remembered that she was wearing a Heartache Melody shirt with the band's logo printed on the chest. She rolled her eyes and played with the strands of her long ponytail.

"It's called being a good manager, promoting the band I manage. Even if their lead singer is a dickhead." Her arctic tone must have gotten to him, or maybe it was the fact she was calling him a dickhead so loud the entire bar could hear them arguing, but his eyes seemed to darken and then he said. "Sing with me."

Andrea staggered back, shaking her head. It was one thing singing in front of him but it was too intimate, too revealing to get on that stage and sing with him. It was a foolish dream that her teenage self had fantasied about, that Declan would be on stage singing and she would come out from the wings and sit down at her piano or with her guitar and join in with him.

Then he would realize the girl of his dreams, the one he wrote songs about in his notebooks had always been there all this time.

It was a stupid childish dream that she had long given up on...hadn't she?

Declan drained the rest of his pint, then headed for the stage before Andrea could do anything to stop him. She was powerless as he rolled his shoulders and sat down behind the piano and tinkled with the keys like he was rusty. Declan was a master at the guitar but it was Andrea and Rhys who had thought him how to play the piano so he would at least not suck and embarrass himself had a passable.

Everyone in the bar, including Andrea, was on the edge of their seats as Declan began to play the keys in earnest, using Andrea's favourite trick of turning a dance song into a classical ballad as he began to sing. His voice was as smooth as silk, but somehow also gritty and raw with emotion as he began to sing the lyrics to David Guetta's remix of the Whitney Houston song, *How will I Know*?

Andrea knew the song, knew the lyrics, where John Newman was singing about hurting, the lyrics being sang to the person about an act that was so bad, the singer wasn't sure if he would know if they really loved him. The way Declan sang it, the power in his voice evoking emotion in Andrea and she hated him for it. In that moment she actually despised him because it felt as if Declan was mocking her, knew what he had done and he was sorry and this was his way of asking her if she cared about him.

But she forced herself to listen, absorbing it all until Declan finished to rapturous applause, yet, she did not clap. Her heart was racing inside her chest and it felt so damn hard to breathe. Her chest tightened and her palms began to sweat as someone handed Declan a guitar, his masterful fingers stroking the chords as he launched into Finneas' *A Concert Six Months From Now.*

Andrea was able to hold her composure until she heard him sing the line about how they never were good at just being friends and the pain inside Andrea seemed to punch its way out. Declan was still singing, his eyes on her but everyone else was watching him.

Struggling to breathe, Andrea bolted out from her spot at the bar and was up the stairs before the music halted suddenly and Declan was calling her name. Andrea kept moving until she pushed open the doors of the student centre and bent over, her hands on her knees as she tried to remember how to take air into her lungs.

The pounding of her heart was so loud in her ears that she didn't hear anyone coming out behind until she finally managed to take a deep breath and it didn't burn like before.

A hand rested on the small of her back and the contact seared her as Declan asked her if she was okay. Andrea jerked away from him, standing upright, aware that her cheeks were wet and she didn't care if he saw it.

"Don't touch me." she snapped at him and Declan looked taken about at the venom in her tone.

"Andi...hey...this was not what I planned."

"Oh, I'm sorry," Andrea snorted, swiping the tears angrily from her eyes. "You didn't show up to embarrass me in front of all my friends? You didn't show up just to torment me? Do you hate me so much that you would come here and pick apart my life?"

Declan shoved his hands into his pockets and sighed. "I didn't mean to embarrass you, Andi. I wanted to talk to you, to try and clear the air. We have to work together and all this animosity isn't good for the band."

Ah so that was it...he was worried about how it was affecting the band. Andrea could solve that for him in an instant. "I'll delegate any personal interaction with the band to a member of my team. You won't have to see me again. there...problem solved."

"That's not what I meant and you know it...give me a fucking break, Andi."

His words were growled, and strained, but his expression was crestfallen, like he didn't know how he had messed up his big gesture so much but Andrea couldn't continue to feel like she was on the cusp of breaking down.

Folding her arms across her chest, Andrea shrugged. "We obviously can't work together so it makes sense to have someone as an intermediary. No point compromising the deal."

Declan scowled as he scrubbed his hand down his face as he remarked in a snarky tone. "You really are a ballbuster, Andi. Fucking hell."

"Seriously? Andi? Your ballbusting, take no prisoner's sister?" Declan said with a whistle through his teeth. "Are you insane?"

Andrea recoiled like Declan had struck her. And there it was the tone and those exact words that had tilted her world on its axis once before but Andrea was no longer that lovestruck girl. She lost her composure, insecurities flooding through her. "Just go home, Declan. How did the boy I knew turn into such a horrible human being? Just because I'm assertive it threatens your manliness? Go fuck yourself, Declan. I'd never treat you this shitty." Andrea turned round and headed back into the student centre as she called over her shoulder. "Just fucking leave me alone."

CHAPTER FOURTEEN

Declan

WEEKS HAD PASSED since Declan made an utter fool of himself and had showed up in Manchester hoping...well, he wasn't sure what he was hoping for but it wasn't the shitshow that had imploded. There was this look at the end of the night, where Andi had looked like he had struck her, that caused this incredible dart of pain in his chest when she told him to leave her alone.

They hadn't spoken in weeks apart from Andi calling to tell the band that Emerald Records was having a charity gala in London and attendance was mandatory. She also told them to dress smart because there would be a lot of eyes on the band, and lots of other musicians would be in attendance. She cited this as being a good opportunity to be asked to open a show for an established artist and really kickstart their success.

Luna had been the one to ask Andi if she would be attending with them and on the video call, Declan watched as she shook her head, telling Luna that she was in the process of handing over management of the band to someone else in Rebel PR so they would be in attendance, not her.

It was only then did Declan speak up, shocking the band when he told Andi that Heartache Melody signed a contract to deal with her and not some lackey she deigned to palm off on them. He grunted at Andi that he was more than happy to call Tim and tell him they wanted out of their deal because Andi wanted to alter the terms of the contract.

Declan felt the weight of the band looking at him with wide eyes as he held Andi's iron stare, her anger palpable even over video link. There was a tense few minutes when he thought Andi would tell him to go for it, but instead, she rolled her eyes and just said fine before she ended the call.

Rhys had words with him after and asked him what the hell he was playing at with his sister. Declan told his best friend that what was going on with him and Andi was none of his business. That had earned him a dark look from Rhys before he told Declan that if he hurt Andi, then Rhys would have no problem breaking his legs, reminding him he didn't actually need his legs to play guitar.

Declan had been inclined to turn down Noah's offer to go-karting but then Noah slyly told him Andi was tagging along as well and Declan heard himself say sure, before his brain could catch up with his mouth.

The day had gotten off to a brilliant start when Declan had tried to be all chivalrous and help Andi into her race suit, zipping it up, and then he had allowed himself to leave his hands on her waist before Andi had growled at him and swatted his hands away.

They were already in their karts when Quinn frowned and they realized they had no marshal. Andi all but leapt from the kart before anyone else could offer, yanking off her helmet and telling everyone that she was quite happy to just stand and watch. Andi went and got a chequered flag and waved it to start the race.

It made him smile under the safety of his helmet at just how sexy Andi looked standing with one hand on her hip as she waved the flag about.

He was so focused on admiring Andi that he had a slow start off the line but he should have known that when he was up against seasoned racers, he had little hope of getting any advantage. The racers made him look like a total amateur and he was.

Declan waited until Charlie stopped racing first then he decided that was enough humiliation for a day. He steered the kart off to the side and got out, just as his phone vibrated in his pocket. He yanked off his helmet, grunted as he strode into the garage, and answered his phone.

"Jay, what's the story?"

"I've just had to bail Rhys out of jail." His friend's rumbled tone came down the line.

Declan let loose an exasperated sigh. Rhys was getting more and more out of control lately and though they all wanted to be rockstars, they didn't want to be hitting the headlines for all the wrong reasons.

"What he do this time?" Declan asked, dreading the answer.

"Tried to be a hero and intervene when some asshole sucker-punched his girlfriend. He was defending her when the guards turned up, and then Rhys swung for one of them thinking it was the boyfriend's buddies. Thankfully it was your brother he took a swing for."

Thank jayus for small mercies.

While his brother Eric was a firefighter, his other brothers were also first responders. Connor was a paramedic and James was a shade, or in politer terms a member of the garda. Rhys was lucky that it was James that he tried to deck and not some fresh meat out of Tullamore looking to make a name for himself.

"You need me to come and have a word?" Declan asked, scrubbing a hand down his face.

"Nah, I've got him at Niamh's shop with me. He's

asleep in the back. I'll give ya a shout if that changes. We owe James a pint."

When the sun finally set and the racers had finished up with their own competition, Charlie ordered food, and Declan sat down beside Andi, eating his food out of the takeaway box. He started to think about ideas for an upcoming video shoot, if the band could agree on which song to release first and he had already asked the racers if they would be in the video but his mind started to go in to overdrive.

"We could always get little kids in to play you lot as karters, the band playing to the side and then fade to you three strutting your stuff." He was super excited about the idea and was thinking maybe when the little kids were karting, they could find little kids to play the band as well when he heard Andi speak.

"We could use kids from the program." Andi mused, pulling out her phone and typing down notes. "Get some publicity for everyone involved."

"Do you ever stop working, woman?" Declan all but growled at Andi.

"You were the one who brought up the damn music video!"

They scowled at each other with Quinn and Luke snapping photos and he was laughing then at a faced Noah pulled before Charlie agreed to take a snap with him and he almost missed Andi getting to her feet and heading outside. Declan was on his feet and chasing after her a second later.

"Andi."

She froze at the sound of her name and slowly, turned to look at him.

"We need to talk about what happened in Manchester."

"We really don't." she retorted with a snort.

"For fuck sake, Andi," Declan shouted, throwing his hands up in the air. "Just tell me what the fuck I did and stop punishing me for something I don't even know about. You owe me that at least."

Andi pointed a finger at him, her lisp twisted into a snarl. "I owe you nothing. But fine, you want to know what you did? What you said? I'll tell you." Declan stood motionless, his heart stuttering as Andi told him why she had ghosted him.

"I heard you, you and Rhys. He asked you the day of the concert if something was going on between us and what was your response? You laughed, Declan. You laughed your head off at the thought that anything would happen between us because of course Rhys was insane to think you'd be interested in his ball-busting, take no prisoners sister. But sure, the concert ticket was free so what harm was it to go with poor, naïve Andi who was falling in-"

Andi clamped her lips shut as Declan wracked his memories for the conversation that she was referring to and then it hit him like a sledgehammer, the nervous way he had deflected Rhys's question knowing he deserved to tell Andi first how he felt about her and he was not about to let Rhys blurt it out and spoil the night.

Turns out Declan had done that all by himself.

He was about to apologize, about to tell Andi just what he had planned to say that night but Andi was already walking away from him and he knew now why she had been so upset in Manchester because he was such a massive asshole that he had used almost the exact same words but to her face this time.

When Declan finally snapped into action, he ran around the building but Andi was already in her car and driving out of the car park and Declan was powerless to do anything but watch her leave.

Chapter Fifteen

Andrea

Two weeks had passed since Andrea had blurted out to Declan about what he had said and she hadn't heard a word. He hadn't texted, he hadn't called...hell, she even wished he would have sent one of those voicenotes that annoyed the hell out of her. But she'd gotten radio silence.

She'd been kept busy though, dealing with a PR nightmare that could have ruined Charlie and Noah's little sliver of happiness. Everything had worked out thankfully, and her and Noah had buried the hatchet so to speak when he thanked her for sorting it and for being a rock to Charlie.

"You're not the witch I thought you were." He had teased.

The broody bastard had even laughed when Andrea joked that she would take payment in the way of their firstborn child.

Andrea hadn't even taken a break the past week and she was exhausted but tonight was the Emerald Records charity gala and she had to attend to get the band there. Luckily enough, her plus one had demanded she take the day off and take to the spa in the hotel, getting pampered before the big night.

JJ had rented out the most expensive suite in the hotel and then booked her in for all kinds of treatments so that by the time the hair and makeup people arrived, she was as relaxed as could be. Her date for the night was dressed in an impeccable tuxedo in a charcoal grey that made his green eyes pop even more.

The team finished with her hair, pulling it back off her face and then letting it fall in a messy curl down her back. Her makeup was very rock chick, with a dark red lip and smokey eyes. And then there was her dress.

JJ had been adamant that he would buy her dress for her, and he wouldn't hear any arguments. When he showed her the dress he had picked out, Andrea had been stunned and told JJ that there was no way in hell that she could pull that dress off.

Dismissing her with the wave of his hand, JJ had asked her just to try it on and after being zipped into the devastating dress, Andrea looked at herself in the mirror and fell in love. The black designer dress was cut at different angles, with a high neck that hugged her throat. Then the material was cut to show off her bare shoulders and arms, a slash at the chest revealing just a tease of her breasts before the dress tapered in to accentuate her curvy hips. The dress was floor-length but had a slit that would have been perilously close to revealing her crotch if not for a slight extra piece of material that preserved her modesty.

JJ had given her this stupid grin when she exited her bedroom and whistled, telling her that if the sight of her didn't make the foolish rock star lose his damn mind, then Andrea needed to forget all about him. Andrea had laughed, shaking her head before she slipped her feet into a pair of black Louboutin's.

Now Andrea was bracing herself for the media, as JJ opened the door to his car and Andrea tried to get out of the car without flashing her knickers. Thankfully JJ held her hand and shielded her getting out of the car as the assembled media shouted for Andrea to tell them who she was wearing, were her and JJ an item, and all that stuff.

Andrea posed with JJ, smiling for a few shots before she stepped aside and let JJ do his thing before he joked that his date was getting cold and ushered her inside. The owner of Emerald Records held the gala at his sprawling country estate in London every year, opening his home to the rich and famous. Andrea had seen pictures online and as someone who came from a three-bed semi-detached house in a middle-class area, Andrea could never understand the need for a house this size when you hardly spent any time there.

JJ place a hand on the small of her back and steered her inside, stopping to greet a few other movie stars and dignitaries, introducing Andrea and they politely smiled at her like she was insignificant until one of England's premier footballs came over and gave Andrea a hug and told the men that she was a goddess and they should hire her whenever they needed a PR rep.

She would be sending him a thank you gift first thing in the morning.

Music drifted out from down the hall and she swayed with the music, JJ noticing and he offered a farewell, then led Andrea down the hall. The house was crammed with people, and Andrea looked around her to see if the band had arrived but couldn't see them just yet.

If the house on the outside looked extravagant, then the inside was even more so. Andrea noted gold handles on doors, pristine marble floors, and that wasn't even the most lavish of it. JJ walked her through an archway and Andrea sucked in a breath.

The record executive had an actual concert hall in his back garden. There were a dozen steps down to a football pitch sized hall that was surrounded by glass. It looked like a massive sunroom but this piece of divinity had a stage at the bottom, where an orchestra played classical versions of recent music. Right now, they were playing a very nice cover the newest single from the girl band Nicolette was managing, and Andrea knew she wanted to get the band in with an orchestra.

"No work tonight, gorgeous."

Andrea rolled her eyes at JJ, glanced at the arm he was holding out to her and then linked her arm in his, grinning up at him as they began their descent down the steps until JJ leaned in to whisper in her ear. "Head up, my love. You have a lot of eyes on you."

Andrea jerked her head up, trying not to scan the room as cameras flashed and JJ held her tightly when her eyes locked with piercing blue eyes and she almost stumbled in her skyscraper high heels. She pulled her eyes from his, just to still her beating heart so that she didn't do a Madonna and tumbled down the stairs.

At the bottom of the stairs, JJ let go of her arm to grab two glasses of champagne and Andrea downed hers, then took JJ's, who quirked a brow at her but didn't say anything. Tim Brett came over and dragged Andrea over to introduce her to a few Emerald Records executives and she offered JJ an apologetic smile even as he waved her off with a wink and disappeared into the crowd.

After a good hour of smoozing, Andrea excused herself to go and find JJ, only to see him deep in conversation with the band and her heart sank. She knew she would have to go and talk to them eventually, but she needed a lot more alcohol to face Declan.

Standing in the middle of the room, she was about to turn around when Rhys spotted her, and came rushing forward, his grin lopsided when meant he'd already had a few too many drinks but even she had to admit the Calvin Klein suit she had sent him looked dashing.

Rhys hugged her and she smelled the whisky on him. "You've been avoiding us all night."

Andrea smacked him on the shoulder. "I've been networking, bro. that's my job. I just spoke to someone in BBC radio all about you lot so this is a business meeting to me."

Rhys linked her arm as he steered her toward the band. "JJ's sound out."

She nudged him with her shoulder but said nothing as Luna was shamelessly flirted with JJ, then winked at Andrea before she came forward and Andrea could see men looking at her. Luna had pulled her blood-red hair back into a severe ponytail, high-lighting her green eyes that twinkled and the stunning smile, with lips that were painted a navy blue to match the dress she wore.

The dress was couture, plastered to her slim but muscular frame, the muscles on her arms exposed from drumming, and her legs, though short were exposed in all their pale glory, with a hem that was short at the front and longer at the back, the material swishing as she moved.

"Andi, your dress...damn girl... if I liked women I would totally try and seduce ya."

While her twin, Luke, was quiet when not plied full of drink, Luna was loud and proud with her thick Cork accent, as the band laughed when JJ looked startled at her forwardness and a politician at the next table nearly spat out his drink.

Andrea grinned, returning her grin as she teased. "Girl same. I've already kissed a girl and didn't like it so it's a shame. We would have made a hot couple."

Chapter Sixteen

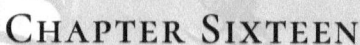

Andrea

Luna laughed as Rhys rolled his eyes and she chatted with Jameson for a few minutes, feeling the weight of Declan's eyes on her before Luna grabbed her arm, her mouth open as she sucked in a breath and mumbled something inaudible.

Andrea was worried Luna was unwell but then Rhys clarified that Luna was actually starstruck because one of the UK's hottest rockstars, who had actually been born in Ireland but had moved to the UK with his English born aristocrat father and had become a hellraiser in the music scene.

And he happened to be one of Andrea's clients.

Without saying anything, she turned around and

put her fingers in her mouth, giving a very loud wolf whistle. The man in question turned around and grinned before surging forward, lifting her off her feet and kissing her hard on the mouth.

Andrea laughed and smacked him hard on the shoulder. "Let me down, you cretin. People will talk."

Oliver Scott or Oli set her down and placed his hands on her hips. "People already talk about me, darling. You look fucking hot as hell."

And so did Oli, who had given a massive FU to the black-tie and shown up with black skinny jeans, dirty boots, and a sleeveless tee that showed off his tattooed arms and neck. He also had an array of piercings and the lobes of his ears were stretched.

"Stop with the flattery and come and meet the band I'm currently managing. You go on tour next year, right?"

Oli chuckled, shaking his head. "Damn, woman do you ever have fun? Take a night off."

"This is fun for me, Oli. We all can't do full rock star and trash hotel rooms."

Rolling his eyes, Oli groaned. "That was one time and if I remember correctly, being wasted and all, it was JJ who started it all."

The JJ in question told Oli his memories were playing tricks on him in his old age, the two of them friends, since they had both, attended the same drama school.

They had walked up to the band now, where Luna

was nearly passed out as Andrea introduced them and then shamelessly told Oli that she would be very upset if he didn't invite the band on tour with him next year.

Oli glanced at the band, then zoned in on Luna. "Luna Sullivan, right? I've seen your socials. Sick videos. Even Milo was impressed." Milo was Oli's drummer and revered in the music industry.

Someone called Oli and he held up his hand in way of farewell. "Andi, call me next week and we can sort out what the story is with the tour." He stopped middle of the floor and then grinned. "Or just call me, day or night. You should spend the night with me and forget all about the actor. You and me could have some wild times, Andi baby!"

JJ erupted with laughter as Andi flashed Oli the middle finger, and just rolled her eyes, ignoring the heated glare from Declan's eyes. Andrea studied him for a minute, and she thought he looked devastating in his all black suit and shirt, the collar unbuttoned to reveal a flash of skin and it suited him because where JJ was refined elegance, Declan was wild masculinity and it was intoxicating.

The lights dimmed and the orchestra slowed the pace of the tempo and Andrea closed her eyes and sighed, relishing in the comfort as the band played the Fray's *Look after You*.

"Shall we dance?"

Andrea opened her eyes slowly to see JJ holding out his hand to her and she slipped her hand into his and let him lead her to the dance-floor. JJ dropped his hands to her waist and Andrea in turn rested her palms on his wide shoulders. They swayed to the music, JJ looking down at her and Andrea knew they looked like any other couple to oblivious eyes, more people gathering around them to dance as well.

"Your Declan had a word with me." JJ mused as he glided them along the dance-floor.

Andrea moved so that she could look over at the table the band was standing at and frowned to see Declan watching them. JJ's hand slipped lower on her waist and she sighed as dragged her gaze away from Declan and back to JJ.

"What did he say?" she asked, not sure if she really wanted to hear it at all.

JJ spun her around, then leaned in closer. "He said that you were one in a million, a sliver of sunshine on a stormy day and if I hurt you, he would come knocking because you deserved to be happy with someone who made you smile instead of cry. It was quite poetic; I can see why he writes lyrics."

"What did you say?"

The words tumbled from her lips as her heart ached because part of her didn't believe he had said such things about her...when all she was used to was his callousness.

"I told him not to worry and that there was more chance of me bedding the younger Collins than the female Collins. That you were a dear friend who helped me keep up a rouse that's very quickly becoming painful." Andrea was shocked that JJ had outed himself to Declan because she was trying to get him to be truthful about who he really was and help him navigate Hollywood as a gay man but so far, he had repeatedly declined.

"Why would you tell him? Why would you give him that?"

JJ looked wistfully at her, then he cupped her cheek. "I am a fucking great actor and I have made it my business to study expressions and body language. No matter what happened in the past, Andi, Declan walks into a room and he sees not a soul but you. I would give anything to have someone look at me the way he looks at you."

"No, he doesn't," she whispered, leaning her head against JJ's broad chest to hide her heated cheeks.

"If this was one of my movies, I would remember the heated blue eyes the moment you started to walk down the stairs and I would mimic it, because your rockstar had this look of pure astonishment as if he was seeing you again for the first time. If that boy isn't in love with you, I'll hand over my first Oscar to you."

That made Andrea laugh as JJ turned her again, the music changing and she sighed, her heart conflicted because no matter how much she denied it, she still had feelings for Declan and while she wasn't certain if, after all this time, she could label it as simply being in love with him, there was and would always be *some-thing* between them...even if she wasn't sure what.

"What do you want, Andi? What would make you happiest?"

That stumped her because no one had ever asked her what would make her happy. She spent most of her time making sure others were happy and content. She worked long hours doing so and while she dated a little, Andrea had never let herself develop feelings, making sure that as soon as things might look like they could be something, she called it quits.

The music changed, David Gray's *This year's love* flooding the room. It was one of her all-time favourite songs and it made her smile, lifting her head from JJ's chest. "I love this song."

JJ leaned down and kissed her cheek. "You deserve to be with a man who knows to request songs that you love."

Andrea narrowed her gaze, wondering what the hell JJ was on about when she heard an achingly familiar rumbled voice say. Can I cut in?"

Stepping back from JJ, aware that there were quite a few eyes on them, Andrea felt her heart race and she tried to remember that she was known for being calm and collected. But this was Declan Walsh who was standing there, asking her to dance with heat in his eyes, and Andrea didn't know if she could recover if she let him take her in his arms, dancing to one of her favourite songs and then they went back to hating one another when reality set in.

The world seemed to disappear as Declan waited for her response and Andrea knew she would eventually say yes, that the girl who wanted to know what it would be like to be loved by the boy who shattered her heart was stronger of will than the woman who told herself she didn't need romance or love in her life, that she was content.

This wouldn't end well for her and as Andrea heard Declan ask one more time, his tone seemed desperate and it occurred to her that they had chosen the perfect name for their band because in the end, the music in her heart would only play a heartache melody and she would be the one destroyed.

CHAPTER SEVENTEEN

Declan

DECLAN'S HEART was in his throat as he saw the indecision flash on Andi's face before she grinned, the smile not quite meeting her eyes as she stepped aside. "Sure, no hassle. JJ would *love* to dance with you."

After his brief conversation with the actor, Declan now knew he was exactly what Andi had told him and not competition for Andi's affections. JJ shook his head as he backed away, mumbling that the two of them were perfect for one another. Andi stood there staring at him then her face fell and she looked like she was about to bolt.

Declan swept forward, forcing Andi to wrap her arms around his neck, his hands pulling her to him the moment he slid them down her body and rested on the curve where her hip and her ass met.

Andi shivered at his touch and it gave him confidence, despite the fact that Declan had two left feet and didn't have a clue what he was doing and he emphasized that by nearly trampling on Andi's very expensive shoes.

"I'm not good at this." He mumbled, pulling Andi flush against his body, almost groaning at how right this felt, having her in his arms finally, where he felt that she belonged if only he could convince her that they were meant to be together.

Andi tilted up her head and it was like being back with the girl who had stolen his heart, who say into his very soul and knew him once again.

"Just imagine we are in your mam's kitchen at 2 am and I'm helping you practise for the dance. Just sway to the music, Declan. You know music, and dancing is just moving to music."

He did as he was told, swaying instead of trying to dance like JJ could, and just held Andi to him, the breath almost leaving his lungs when she rested her head against his chest and when the song changed, she heard her sing softly along with the melody and he fell all over again.

"Your heart is racing." His Andi remarked, lifting her head to look up at him and he tried to tell her with his expression exactly why.

"It's because after all these years, you're here in my

arms and I don't want to let you go. I made a stupid childish mistake and it cost me the chance to be with you."

Andi sighed and dipped her eyes. "That's all in the past."

"It's not for you, Andi, because I can see how much I hurt you. I said it, I admit that but I didn't mean it. I was trying to play it cool in front of Rhys, because you were always so private and I didn't want to tell your brother that I was in love with you before I told you."

Stumbling back, Andi shook her head and when Declan went to take her in his arms again, she let him but couldn't help the way her body stiffened. He wanted to tell her everything and this was his chance, his shot at redemption.

Declan trailed his hands down her back and rested them dangerously close to her spectacular ass in that dress and he almost punched the air when Andi bit down on her bottom lip.

"You don't have to lie just to make me feel better, Declan...we can ...we can just be friends."

"I don't just want to be friends with you, Andi." He heard himself growl, lowering his lips to her ear. "I want to spend hours learning all of you with my mouth, my hands, my tongue. I want to worship you like I should have done before I fucked it up. I want to spend lazy Sunday mornings with you naked in my bed, your smile and maybe those heels the only thing that you are wearing."

Andi leaned back, pink flushing her cheeks as she frowned. "Stop."

But Declan wasn't prepared to stop. "I never could sleep in your house once I released that I wanted you, knowing you were lying in the bed just behind the wall. I fantasied about sneaking into your bedroom, waking you up with a kiss, and doing everything a horny teenager wanted to do with the girl who haunted his mind."

Andi looked shocked by his admissions but then she surprised him by loosening her grip on the back of his neck and placing her palms against the column of his neck, heat in her eyes as she said. "I used to stroke myself to sleep, wishing you would come in and finish what I started. I swear my mind played tricks on me because there were nights when I had my fingers buried inside me that I felt you outside my room and I would orgasm so hard that I had to bite my lip to stop from screaming."

Declan hissed out a breath, his cock hardening and he pulled Andi flush against him so she could feel just how affected he was by her. "I was but I never knew...if I'd known...I'd have...fuck Andi. I want inside of you so bad, wanted to devour you since I saw you walk in dressed in that dress and it's driving me insane."

He lowered his lips to graze the skin at her neck, and Andi buried her face in his chest to cover the sound of her moan and it made his cock throb. He flicked out his tongue, tasting her skin for the first time and it was like a revelation like he had found the perfect melody to go with the lyrics he had penned.

Andi's hands slipped down from his neck to the expanse of his chest and he kissed her neck, teasing her, tempting her to follow through with this combustible chemistry between them, for him to take her back to his hotel room and not leave for days.

Then Andi placed her palms firmly on his chest and pushed him away gently, her eyes no longer heated but sad.

"Andi..." Declan started, reaching for her again. But Andi was shaking her head as if trying to clear her thoughts.

"No...this is...we can't. This doesn't change anything. My body might still want you but I can't forget everything. Only a couple of weeks ago you tossed back at me that I was a ballbuster. I am. And you are a cocky rockstar who thinks he wants the one girl who he never could have."

It broke his heart that he thought that was all between them.

It angered him as well that she would cheapen his feelings.

"Is that all you think this is? That I only want you because we never got together."

Andi offered him a small smile. "That's all it is...a stupid infatuation. Once you got me out of your system, you would go back to being Declan Walsh, Irish rock god in the making where women would get wet the moment you started to sing and I can't ...I don't think I'd survive it. This was a terrible idea."

Declan knew the moment Andi was going to walk away from him and panic surged through him. He needed to tell her that there would never be another woman for him, that any woman he had slept with over the years had paled in comparison to her, that when he looked at her, he saw his future and he had never stopped loving her even when he told himself that he didn't deserve it.

Andi made to pass by him, her eyes filled with tears but Declan snapped out his hand and caught her roughly on the arm. "Don't walk away from me, Andi. Not again. Don't you fucking dare."

Declan was fully aware that the entire room had fallen silent, even the music had stopped and were now watching them. Both JJ and Oliver Scott made to come forward but they stopped when they took stock of whatever dark look was stamped on his face.

"Let go of me, Declan." Andi's voice was calm, emotionless and he knew she was asking him to let her go, to leave her alone and he couldn't do that.

"I can't do that, Andi. I let you walk away once and I refuse to do it again. I can't."

Andi yanked her arm out of his grasp, her eyes darting around in embarrassment as she realized everyone was watching their interaction and she looked dejected, and he knew he was to blame for it and he hated himself for it.

He opened his mouth to apologize, to ask her to talk, to go to some quiet place, just the two of them, and get everything off their chests. He never got the chance to because out of nowhere, a fist connected with his jaw and knocked him to his knee, pain blooming in his face as Declan glanced and saw the enraged face of his best friend whose lips were curled in a vicious snarl.

"Don't you fucking put hands on my sister!"

Chapter Eighteen

Andrea

Under normal circumstances, Andrea would have been flattered by Rhys's attempt at defending her honour but tonight it just made her hella mad. When Declan got to his feet, wiping the blood from his cut lip off with the sleeve of his jacket and Rhys took another menacing step toward Declan, Andi stepped in between them and placed her palms out to keep them separated.

"Rhys, go and get some fresh air and calm the fuck down. You are embarrassing me and I swear to all that is holy that I will drag your ass out of here by the ear if you don't walk away now."

She knew her brother was wasted by the bloodshot

eyes and the slight sway as he tried to stand still but there was this blanket of darkness in his eyes as he looked from Declan to her.

"I knew it. All those years I knew you two had feelings for one another. I tried to pretend it wasn't happening every time you both lied to my face that you were just friends." Rhys snorted, his gaze narrowing. "Did he tell you that he went out and slept with the first available girl the night you stood him? That he hadn't cared enough to try and get you to explain to him. He just went out and got drunk and fucked the first bitch that offered to suck him off."

Nausea rolled in her stomach and she felt the urge to be sick, knowing it was the truth. And yet, this was more humiliating that knowing that Declan's first reaction was to go and get laid. She felt the man in question sag under her palm and she tried to hold back her tears.

Andrea felt one of the traitorous tears slip-free, slowly trickling down her face and it was when Rhys suddenly snapped out of his angry drunken haze and looked devastated that he had made her cry.

"Jaysus, Andi...I'm sorry."

Andrea didn't think she could respond to her brother as she dropped her hands and felt like she might faint, her chest tightening with panic.

Then, like a dark angel to her rescue, she heard the unmistakable sound of Oli screaming into his microphone as someone hammered on the drums, and attention turned from the shitshow of her life to the unbelievable duet that was happening on stage.

Had she not been utterly broken inside, she might have marveled at the distraction Oli was no doubt providing for her, Luna on the drums as JJ strode across the dance-floor, wrapped an arm around her waist and all but carried her from the party.

She didn't care what Declan and Rhys did once she left, ignored the buzzing of her phone as she stared out the window of JJ's car and couldn't bear the weight on her chest. It felt like she was watching herself from outside her body and wanted to scream at herself for letting herself let Declan shatter her heart for the second time.

"I can call Charlie...if you need to talk to her." JJ offered but Andrea just shook her head. Her best friend was happy with her race car driver in Australia and they were prepping for the first race of the season and didn't need to deal with all the drama.

Surely it would be all over the news in about an hour and when Charlie woke up, she would call the moment she saw it. Besides, Andrea wasn't sure she had the mental capacity to truly explain the massive fucking dent in her career tonight would have done.

Because her career was the only thing she might salvage from the ruins of tonight.

If Heartache Melody could even function as a band after everything.

Andi was so out of it that she barely knew what

was happening as JJ brought her up to their suite and went to fix her a cup of tea. She kicked off her heels and just stood in the middle of the sitting area that separated the two bedrooms and replayed the events over in her mind.

"I want to spend hours learning all of yours with my mouth, my hands, my tongue. I want to worship you like I should have done before I fucked it up. I want to spend lazy Sunday mornings with you naked in my bed, your smile and maybe those heels the only thing that you are wearing."

"I was trying to play it cool in front of Rhys, because you were always so private and I didn't want to tell your brother that I was in love with you before I told you."

"I never could sleep in your house once I released that I wanted you, knowing you were lying in the beds just behind the wall. I fantasied about sneaking into your bedroom, waking you up with a kiss, and doing every-thing a horny teenager wanted to do with the girl who haunted his mind."

The pressure of his hand on her arm as Declan snarled. "Don't walk away from me, Andi. Not again. Don't you fucking dare."

"I didn't want to tell your brother that I was in love with you before I told you."

Andrea let loose the sob she had been holding in so suddenly that JJ dropped the mug of tea and it crashed to the ground, and it was as if the mug was a metaphor for just how shattered Andrea felt. She suddenly couldn't breathe and she blindly clawed at her throat, tears blurring at her throat as she heard Declan's sultry voice in her ear. *"Fuck Andi. I want inside of you so bad, wanted to devour you since I saw you walk in dressed in that dress and it's driving me insane."*

She tried to reach around to unzip her dress but her hands were shaking too much and then she heard herself hysterically begging JJ to get it off, to get the dress off of her because she couldn't breathe, couldn't think.

Andrea gulped in air as JJ yanked down the zipper and she heard the material rip as JJ tried to get it off of her as fast as he could and then, she was stepping out of the damned dress and standing in the suite, in her underwear having what was probably a nervous breakdown.

Her hands were clutched to her chest as she let loose a frustrated scream, then gave way to more sobs as she crumpled to the ground, her knees giving out, and then JJ was pulling her into his lap as she cried and cried and cried for gods knows how long.

JJ rocked her back and forth, caressing her hair and murmuring softly to her that everything would be okay and that everything would be better in the morning.

Andrea sure as shit didn't believe him one bit.

Her eyes became super heavy and she must have dozed off because she darted awake when she felt herself being jostled, JJ carrying her to her room and laying her down on the bed. Her eyes lowered instantly the moment her head hit the pillow and she felt the warmth off JJ's lips as he kissed her forehead before stepping outside.

Hours or minutes later, Andrea heard voices outside and then the door opened for a second before it was left slightly ajar, a sliver of light creeping through the darkened room.

"I dunno, Charlie. I've never seen her like this. It's like she's just given up."

"Do you need me to come back?" Her best friend asked, probably on a video call with JJ. "Declan called Noah in bits so it must be bad. I can get on the next flight home."

Andrea loved her best friend for her willingness to drop everything to come to her but as she sat up in the bed, ready to tell Charlie she would be okay, she couldn't bring herself to say the words, merely listened as JJ told Charlie that he would keep his eye on her and let her know if things got worse than they already were.

"Listen JJ, Declan asked Noah if I knew where you guys were staying and while Noah knows that I do, he lied and told Declan I had no clue. If he asks a paparazzi, they might tell him so be prepared in case he does rock up."

"I don't think we have to worry about that, Charlie. The paps know that if they spill my location to anyone, I'll become less willing to pose for pictures and give them soundbites. I'll keep our girl safe...even if I have no clue how to mend her broken heart."

That made fresh tears burn her eyes and she tried to cry as quietly as possible but JJ heard her and came in to lay beside her on the best and simply brushed her hair as she cried, before telling her that he would give anything to stop her hurting.

Well, at least she wasn't the only one who had no clue how to cease the heartache melody in her chest.

CHAPTER NINETEEN

Declan

DECLAN STILL HADN'T RECOVERED from the events of the gala and had shut himself away for days in the studio just pouring his heart and soul into his music, his lyrics. But Andi was never far from his mind and he had picked up his phone a dozen times to call her, staring at the screen for hours not having enough courage to call or text in case she wouldn't answer him.

And then there was Rhys. He'd been a mess since the gala, horrified that he had caused his sister, who Declan knew he adored, so much pain that she had been MIA for days and they would have been worried if Charlie hadn't called Rhys and told him that Andi just needed some time.

Today, they were all gathered in Sullivan's pub to watch the Australian Grand Prix live, the bar closed to all those but family and friends. The place was sombre even as everyone chatted and tried to pretend that nothing had happened. Hell, even Rhys lingered close to the bar, watching Luna with nothing but a coke in front of him.

Declan was so caught up in his own drama that he didn't notice Luna spiraling until Jameson nudged him and inclined his head for her to go and talk to Luna. Her nails tapped against the bar as she worried on her lip and kept her green eyes on the tv screen and the rain that was coming down in torrents on the screen.

"Hey, you doing okay?" he asked Luna and she turned her gaze to his for a second before looking back at the TV.

"I have a bad feeling, Deco. I can't shake the feeling that something is gonna happen to Luke."

Declan reached over, pulled her up so that she was sat on top of the bar. and hugged her, telling her that it was just a feeling and Luke knew what he was doing. She smiled, nodding her head but he could see that she wasn't reassured.

But Declan stayed beside her, Luke's dad Mick behind the bar but the twin's mam couldn't bring herself to watch Luke's race. The noise in the bar quietened down as the lights all flashed red and then blinked out and the race began.

Noah dove down the inside line, getting into second place before the cars had even come to the first corner because the other cars had been slow off the line. The bar cheered when Luke managed to get ahead by two places, everyone grinning when they played Luke's whoop of joy coming down the radio as he got up to P5.

But the rain came down heavier and heavier with all the drivers complaining about visibility. Luke was driving his socks off, and for a while, it looked like both drivers might have a shot at a podium place. Declan glanced over at Luna, who was still watching with this look of apprehension on her face.

Now Declan didn't know a great deal about driving a car at those kinds of speeds but he knew that the cars sliding and struggling to stay on the race track was never a good thing. Luna grabbed his arm, digging her nails into his flesh but he didn't care.

Yesterday, during qualifications, Luke had been having issues with one of the other drivers who had been driving like an idiot and putting everyone on the race track in danger, and today, the stupid asshole was back at it.

Luke was about to lap the other driver, the blue lights flashing to make the driver let Luke by and they all watched in horror as Luke tried to overtake him and the driver cut across Luke unwilling to let Luke get by, clipping the wheel as Luke drove full speed in his attempt to overtake.

The action blew Luke's tire and Luna was already screaming before Luke was struck again and then Declan hauled Luna over the counter, forcing her to not look at the screen and refusing to let her go as she continued to scream, the sounds muffled by his chest.

But Declan watched in absolute horror as Luke's car flipped, rolling like it was in slowly before it smashed into the barrier, the wrong way around, upside down, with Luke still inside of it.

The TV camera moved from the crash site and everyone watching heard as Luke's race manager Tony asked on the radio if Luke was okay and it chilled the blood in his veins when there came no response.

"I'd know if he was dead...I'd feel it, right...he's my twin."

Declan heard the heartbreak in her tone as the ads came on and he let Luna go, and she immediately pulled out her phone and called Quinn, the Rebel Racers reserve driver like a sister to Luke and Luna but she didn't answer. Then she tried Charlie, who also didn't answer.

Declan could do nothing but hold Luna as Mick excused himself to go and tell his wife what was happening as the bar stood in stunned silence and waited for any news on their friend.

The coverage went back to the presenters who gave them an update, their faces grim.

"If you are only just joining us, we have a brief update on the events that just happened. Luke Sullivan was involved in a collision and his crash crashed into a steel barrier. The race has been red-flagged and medical personnel have extracted Luke from his car. The other driver involved has sustained no injuries and the cause is being investigated. That is all the information we have available at his time but updates will be provided as we get them".

The camera moved to one of the former F1 drivers who looked visibly upset as he spoke. "Noah Donovan was first on the scene and tried to get to his friend and teammate until the medical personnel arrived. I think the race should be stopped. If it was me, I wouldn't want to go back on track after that but it's easy for me to say standing here."

They went to another break as Luna tried frantically to get in touch with Quinn, who refused to answer as Luna vented her frustration. "For fuck sake, Quinn...answer the goddamn phone and screw your stupid idiotic pact."

What bloody pact was she on about?

Rhys came over and hugged Luna from behind and rested his chin on her shoulder. "They have a pact; Luke, Noah, and Quinn that if any of them is in an accident, they do not answer to family or friends until they know what the story is. Quinn won't answer her phone until she can tell Luna for certain how Luke is."

They all looked back at the screen as the presenter started to speak. "Okay, so we do have an update with regards to the race. Luke Sullivan has been taken to a local trauma centre and emergency services are doing all they can at the moment. The race will restart in thirty minutes and the Rebel Racers team has made the decision not to continue as they will be going to the hospital to remain with Luke."

The TV was shut off as Mick came out from the back, his eyes red and Luna started trembling as Mick held up his hand for silence. Declan made sure that he was standing beside Luna in case the news was as bad as that crash looked.

"I just got off the phone with Charlie and Tony. Luke is alive but in a critical condition and they have already had to use emergency measures to keep his heart going." Mick's voice broke and the man was visibly shaken. Declan admired his strength for even being able to stand there and speak. "But my boy is strong and a fighter. Now, I need to organize and get myself, the wife, and Luna to Oz so we can see for ourselves that Luke is okay."

Luna's legs gave way and Declan and Rhys caught her as before she went down and Declan lifted her up on to the bar, letting Rhys embrace her as Jameson got the faraway look he got whenever he heard about car accidents so Declan squeezed his shoulder as he passed by to go up to Mick.

"You need me to sort flights, Mick? Anything I can do to help."

Mick gripped his shoulder, and nodded. "You're a good lad, Declan. A good lad."

Declan didn't know want else to say as Mick came over and took his daughter in his arms and the damn broke, with Luna's pained sobs punching a hole in his gut. He strode over to Rhys, who was pale, himself and Luke firm friends as well, and held out his hand.

"Gimmie your phone."

Rhys handed it over without question but his gaze narrowed when he saw him pull up Andi's number and then he asked Declan what he was doing.

"We need flights to Oz asap and who else do we know who can make shit happen."

Then he was dialing the number, his heart in his throat as he heard Andi answer the phone, her voice so sad he almost forgot why he had called. "Andi, it's me...please don't hang up. I need your help."

CHAPTER TWENTY

Andrea

ANDREA HAD GOTTEN out of the bed she had remained in for days the moment Declan explained what had happened and half an hour later, thanks to a quick call to Charlie, she had chartered a plane to Australia. She hadn't intended on going, but Charlie has asked her to come to make sure the Sullivans were looked after. What she hadn't been expecting was for Declan to be in Manchester for the flight as well.

She had tried to hold her nerve, to drag herself from this melancholy that had seemed to settle in her bones. Declan had frowned when his eyes had landed on her and he knew she looked a state but in the grand scheme of things, her broken heart was of little consequence.

Andrea had expected to put back up her walls

where Declan was concerned but then he had to show her why she had fallen in love with him all those years ago he just had to show her why she had fallen in love with him all those years ago.

Luke and Luna's parents had sat quietly at the back of the plane, not saying a word as Declan made sure Luna, who looked absolutely devastated, her eyes red and puffy, was okay. She curled up on the plush chairs on the plane, her head resting on Declan's thigh as he stroked her hair, tears in her eyes. Declan sang at a low murmur, the words barely audible but it make the hair on her arms stand up. Declan kept on singing long after Luna had cried herself to sleep.

Andrea kept to herself in her seat across the way, trying to ignore the way Declan kept lifting his gaze and trying to catch her eye. After an hour of fooling herself that she could get any work done, Andrea closed her laptop and rubbed her eyes. Declan yawned and craned his neck but didn't make a move in case he woke Luna.

Getting to her feet, she went and poured him a cup of coffee, added two sugars, and brought it over to him. The smile he gave her made her stomach flutter and her heart beat, their fingers grazing as he took it from her.

"Cheers." He said, taking a sip before he continued. "I was gasping and too afraid to move in case I disturbed her. She hasn't slept since the crash. Just keeps ringing Luke's phone to hear his voice on the mailbox."

Declan stroked down her hair, smiled, and then lifted those steely blue eyes to her once again.

"I always wanted a little sister." Andrea heard the smile in his tone, in his eyes and she wondered if he ever spoke of her with such warmth in his tone when she wasn't around. "From the moment she walked into our audition, with her fuck you attitude and my balls are bigger than yours swagger, I knew she was special. I would give anything to take her pain away right now and carry it for her."

Andrea, despite everything, reached over and took his hand in hers. "She is asleep now because she knows you are protecting her. She knows you want to keep her safe."

"Jesus, Andi...if Luke's not...if he..."

"Stop." Andrea chided him, wishing that there was not this chasm of distance between them. "Luke will pull through. He has to. We have to have faith that Luke is as much of a fighter as his twin. Until then, we've got her."

Declan studied her for a couple of heartbeats so intently that she pulled her hand from his and then didn't know what to do. Declan shifted slightly, careful not to jostle Luna as he assessed her.

"I don't know how to bring up the fact that you look as tired as Luna without you closing down on me. I know that I did this to you. I hate that no matter what I say, no matter what I try to make amends for, I keep screwing up and I'm pushing you further and further away."

"Dec-" Andrea began before Declan cut across her.

"No...Let me get this off my chest and then it's all out in the open. What I said to Rhys, I said as a stupid, idiotic boy who was trying to cover up the fact he was insanely in love with his best friend's sister who, to be fair, was far too good for him. Still is."

Andrea tried to look away, to shield herself from the emotions in his eyes and the tears from slipping from hers.

"I was shitting myself that I hadn't read the signs. That you didn't feel the same and me bearing my heart would just fracture the friendship we had. But I was planning on telling you that night. I swear on my father's soul, I was."

Andrea was already emotionally strung out and her head was pounding. She knew that Declan was waiting for her to respond, to offer him some sort of absolution but the hostess came and advised them they would land soon and Andrea returned to her seat, feeling Declan's eyes on her as he roused Luna so she could sit upright for the landing.

She had to be there now for the family so Andrea pushed all thoughts of Declan from her mind as the family looked at her with expectant eyes as they disembarked the plane and headed for the blacked-out privacy windowed SUV because there was a rush of media waiting.

Declan shielded Luna from the cameras until they were inside the SUV and driving to the hospital, pulling up to a back entrance where Noah and Charlie waited for them. Just like Declan, Noah took Luna in his arms the moment she got out of the car and Charlie went to the twin's parents.

They all moved through the hospital with an anticipation that felt suffocating, Charlie bringing them to a fancy private family room where a doctor was waiting and he rose, offering a sombre greeting.

Andrea made to step outside, not wanting to intrude on a family moment when she heard Charlie say. "I'd like it if Andi could stay if that's okay Mr. and Mrs. Sullivan. If she doesn't mind, I'd like for her to handle any requests from the media while you guys are here."

The Sullivans nodded grimly as the doctor began to explain the extent of Luke's injuries and that he was at present in an induced coma to try and give his body time to recover. Andrea listened as the doctor explained that Luke surviving the initial forty-eight hours proved how tough he was and that for now, he just needed to rest his body until he was ready.

"When will my son wake up? When will I see his beautiful smile?"

The doctor took hold of Mr's Sullivan's hands and offered her a smile. "My team and I are doing all that we can to make that happen as soon as Luke is ready. You have my word that we are doing everything we possibly can."

"Can we see him? He's my twin and I.... I..." Luna burst into tears and that set her mother off and even Andrea had a massive lump in her throat as Noah and Declan helped Luna to her feet and took her from the room, no doubt taking her to see her brother, her parents, and the doctor following after them.

The door closed behind them and that left her alone with Charlie, who looked like she'd running on empty for days and she probably had.

"Well, girlfriend, you look like shit." Andrea teased trying to ease some of the tension when it worked and Charlie barked out a laugh.

"Right back at ya, bitch." Charlie said as she embraced Andrea. "Thank you for coming. I know you are dealing with some stuff right now but god, I needed you."

They separated, and Andrea hugged herself as they walked out and down the nearly empty corridor. Any doctors or nurses they passed inclined their heads, but it looked like Luke was staying in a quieter part of the hospital.

She and Charlie discussed making a statement to the press, once they had gotten clearance from the family, Charlie knowing that all the Luke Sullivan fans would want to know how their fave driver was doing.

They reached the hospital room and although

Andrea knew it was bad, she had to turn away at the sight of the battered and bruised young man in the bed, the sound of his sister's sobs too much for her to bear witness to. She thought of the happy smiling man who made her feel so welcome and she felt her eyes water.

Andrea wondered how she had let herself wallow over the events of the past few weeks and chastised herself, knowing that life was tragically short and sometimes brutal, as she looked at the boy in the bed and the grief-stricken family, did the insignificant matter of her foolish heart matter at all?

CHAPTER TWENTY-ONE

Declan

THE DAY after they arrived in Australia, the decision was made for the racers to head off to Bahrain for the next race. Noah and Quinn both had been stubborn that they wanted to stay but Mick Sullivan told them that Luke would be spitting fire if he knew they had sat on their asses by his bedside and not gone racing.

Andi planned to stay behind after giving a brief statement to the media about Luke, but Noah had taken her aside, Andi's eyes widening before she nodded her head and gave Noah a genuine smile before she said something that made Noah laugh.

Then Noah was pulling him into an empty hospital room and Declan had quirked his brow.

"I've seen enough medical dramas to know what goes on in an empty room, mate. But you ain't my type."

Noah had barked out a laugh, telling him to fuck off, running his fingers through his hair before he asked Declan to come to Bahrain with Andi in a few days his friend explained to him what he wanted to do, and then Declan was grinning and hugging the other man. When Noah asked him if he thought he was insane, proposing to Charlie so soon, with everything going on, Declan had shaken his head and told Noah that he and Charlie were always meant to be and whether it was now or in a few years, this day was always going to happen.

Declan asked Noah what Andi had said, unable to stop himself from asking and Noah grinned before he said. "Andi told me it was about time I sorted my shit out and that if I ever dared to hurt Charlie in any way, she would bury my body in places no one would ever find me."

That had made Declan grin at the fierce protective woman who had his heart.

Charlie didn't know that he and Andi would be following to Bahrain, so they said a teary goodbye, and then that left just him and her to travel to the new country the next day. Andi spent the entire time on the phone to JJ, updating him on what was going to happen. Declan no longer felt the burn of jealously, considering the other man had contacted him to tell him he was an idiot and to do something, or someone would find a way to break down Andi's walls and treat her in the manner she deserved.

On the Wednesday night, Declan had managed to get his hands on an acoustic guitar and practiced his part of Noah's epic proposal until his fingers ached. He wanted this to be perfect for Noah and Charlie, a little sliver of happiness in the darkest of times.

"Do you need anything else?"

Andi's voice broke through his thoughts and he lifted his head to smile at her. They hadn't spoken much since the plane, he just made sure she had eaten and even slept a little. He opened his mouth to speak when Quinn called Declan and told him he needed to get to the track.

There was a chair waiting for him in the darkness, with Andi hiding just behind the pit wall, her phone poised ready to record this moment for the happy couple. It made him wonder how he would propose to Andi, would he do it on stage, in front of thousands to show her just how much he loved her or would he want to do it in private.

Jesus, Declan was getting a little ahead of himself, wasn't he?

When Charlie and Noah walked hand in hand over the crest of the hill, he froze, not wanting to move in case he spoiled the surprise, lifting his gaze and seeking out the eyes of the girl he couldn't get out of his veins, and it sent a thrill through him that when he looked at her, Andi was already looking right at him, holding his gaze for a moment before she jerked her gaze away.

The couple came to a halt exactly where they needed to be and Declan couldn't help the grin from curving up his lips as Noah faced Charlie, taking her face in his hands.

"Do you trust me?" Noah said to Charlie and her response was immediate.

"With my life, with my heart."

"Close your eyes, Charlotte."

At that Charlie frowned, no doubt suspicious as to what the hell was going on but she did as he asked. Then Noah put his hands on her hips and shifted her so that she could see all that Noah had done to prove his love for the girl who almost got away.

"Open your eyes, Charlotte."

That was his cue to get his performance underway and the moment Charlie opened her eyes, Declan closed his, letting Joy Division's, *Love Will Tear Us Apart* carry across the racetrack. He almost didn't get to witness the romantic moment, but when the song was done, Declan opened his eyes, his fingers still playing as Noah told Charlie.

"I have been in love with you, Charlotte Coyle, since I came crashing into your life and you welcomed me with open arms. I have loved you since and every day I fall harder in love with you. life is short, life isn't predictable but I know, that I don't want to spend a second of it without you."

Declan lifted his gaze to Andi, and it was as if Noah was saying the words that were tattooed into his soul, and would be there long after he was dust on the wind. Andi swiped tears from her eyes, totally focused on the couple, but as if she felt him watching her, she let her gaze drift to his and Declan knew he still had a chance to not fuck it up any more than he already had.

"I want the whole dream with you, Charlie." Noah continued, his voice even and calm, "I want the wedding, the kids, the career. I want to spend Sundays cheering on little girls with green eyes as they whizz around a karting track. I want to be what we never had, a complete family. But I only want that with you. So, Charlotte Coyle, even though you are far more than I will ever deserve, will you marry me?"

"Yes. Of course, it's a yes."

Noah slipped the ring on her finger, then got to his feet, kissing her and twirling her around in his arms as a rapturous amount of applause rang out around them. Charlie had rosy cheeks as everyone cheered and congratulations shouted their way, her eyes filling with tears.

Then Andi stepped out onto the track with her phone held up, waving the phone as she grinned, winking at her best friend. They embraced and then the celebrations got underway, with Declan setting aside his borrowed guitar, grabbing a bottle of non-alcoholic bubbly, and popping the cork to celebrate along with them.

Charlie strode over, pulling Declan into a warm hug and thanking him for the song, and he, in turn, thanked her for giving Noah a second chance. He kissed her cheek, ignoring the playful shove from his friend with a chuckle. Then Noah kissed his fiancé and the entire racetrack cheered.

Later, Declan found himself standing off to the side, watching Andi as she admired Charlie's ring, discussing plans for the wedding and then Andi's phone rang and they held up the phone, obviously showing someone on the video call Charlie's ring.

"I owe you more than a pint, Deco."

Declan had been so engrossed in staring at Andi that he hadn't seen the man of the hour walk up to him, leaning against the barrier beside him. "It was nothing. Call it an early engagement present. Saves me having to shell out for some expensive cutlery or whatever the fuck people buy for presents these days."

Noah laughed, shaking his head, then he sobered. "I never thought I'd be here, engaged to Charlie. After everything I did...after all the shit... and now, fuck...this is what happiness feels like, isn't it?"

Declan didn't know how to answer Noah, just sighed as the other man pushed off the wall, and looked him dead in the eye. "You haven't screwed it up entirely yet, Deco. If me and Charlie can get through what we have, you and Andi can. Isn't it about time you went and got your girl?"

Noah left him then to stew in his thoughts,

annoying Declan as deep down he knew the smug bastard was right. He had hesitated to tell Andi just how much he was in love with her once and it had almost killed him when she left and they were at breaking point now.

Declan knew that no matter what, he wasn't about to let Andi walk away from him this time without a fight. They would confront the past, head-on, and it would either end up as one of his greatest hits or be the biggest flop he'd ever created.

Chapter Twenty-Two

Andrea

THE PROPOSAL and the race after had been thrilling and perfect, and Andrea was deliriously happy for her best friend. It had been a blissful few days away from Ireland and she and Declan had even managed to stay civil to one another...in fact, Declan had been acting the perfect gentleman, making sure she had eaten, rested, and even shrugged off his hoody and given it to her when she was cold one evening.

Andrea had been reluctant to take it, to be drowned in the scent of him, and even now, days after, when she closed her eyes, she could still smell him, and the lingering scent of his Boss aftershave. She knew that she would never not get a whiff of the eau de parfum and not think of Declan.

The band was due to have a recording session in the studio so they could send the executives at Emerald Records evidence that they were in fact working toward a release. Declan had tried to persuade Luna to stay with Luke but she had been adamant about coming back after hearing that there was no set timeline for when Luke might wake up and that for now he couldn't be moved.

The flight home had passed in a blur, with tiredness drowning them all and even Declan had fallen asleep, his head lolling to the side with his arms folded across his chest. Andrea had sat across the way, only getting up to drape a blanket over him when he shivered

Luna, who had been watching the interaction, flashed Andrea a small smile even as Andrea's face had heated in embarrassment. Luna beckoned her over and she went because the girl had been through an ordeal and Andrea couldn't in that moment figure out a way to avoid her.

The moment Andrea took a seat opposite Luna, the girl leaned on her fist and sighed. "You know he's in love with you, right? Has been since before I knew him."

"I don't think that's any of your business, Luna."

Luna laughed, rolling her eyes. "Ya, I know. But still. He is a handsome bastard when he's not scowling and broody, and he doesn't date. He is married to his music because the girl he loves won't give him the time of day and he thinks he doesn't deserve to be happy."

Andrea hadn't responded to Luna's words, but her heart started to race at the thought that Declan wasn't dating. It was hard to believe that someone who looked like him, who sang like him, who was the subject of lots of admiration, hadn't acted on it. Andi knew he was as Luna put it, married to his music, but she never expected him to be a monk.

"He looks after us all and we want him to be happy. I want all my brothers, blood and not, to be happy. If the last few days have taught me anything, it's that life is too damn short to not do, or be with who makes you happy. Luke has hidden a part of himself from the entire world and now..... well now he might never get the chance to find that person who loves him unconditionally."

Andrea had spent a lot of time thinking about what Luna had said and it had kept her awake at night. How could she trust that if she let herself try with Declan that he wouldn't rip her heart out and stomp on it all over again She had turned into a hot mess after the events of the gala, and if she allowed herself to be with Declan, and it all fell apart, knowing what it was like to be loved by Declan, only to lose him all over again might just destroy her.

Pushing that train of thought firmly out of her mind, Andrea got out of her car and strode toward

Declan's home and studio. He had sent her the code to the door yesterday so she keyed it in and stepped inside. Glancing up the stairs, she was tempted to go up and see exactly how Declan was living.

Instead, she opted for the professional approach walking toward the studio and opening the glass door, letting herself in, marveling at the space Declan had created. The area she stood in had two couches facing one another, a low table in between that had scattered music sheets all over it. A beautiful array of guitars were displayed along the wall and someone had painted the walls a dark grey, a smattering of musical quotes decorating them.

There was a kitchenette area also, and there was a collage of pictures of the band. Andrea smiled looking at pictures of Luna and Jameson as youngsters and her smile dropped when she brushed her fingers over a picture of her and Declan, taken maybe about six months before things had gone to shit.

She herself was looking at whoever was taking the picture, maybe Rhys, a pencil tucked behind her ear, laughter in her eyes, and a bright smile curving her lips. But Declan wasn't looking at the camera; he was looking at her with an expression Andrea had never seen before and it made her heart ache.

Turning away from the reminders of the past, Andrea's eyes scanned the room, wondering why no one else was here. The band had been told to be at the studio by ten so they could talk some before getting down to some recording. She had waited until nearly ten to arrive to avoid being alone with Declan but now she realized she was the first one to arrive. Or so she thought.

Something made her walk toward the door that led to the recording booth and Andrea quietly opened the door and went inside. Booth was an understatement. This was a full-out studio set up complete with a separate booth for laying down vocals, and a larger one for band performances. Declan was standing with his back to her, dressed in shorts and a tee, as she listened to the sound of Oliver Scott's patented screaming on a song that was heavy and Andrea instantly loved the beat.

Ducking out of view as Declan moved to lean against a wall and scribbled lyrics hastily before turning to them out, her eyes were drawn to the stunner in the other booth and she just had to go and run her fingers along the beauty.

A baby grand lingered lonely in the rehearsal space, a stark black against the ivory keys, and Andrea slipped into the booth and traced her fingers along the top of the sleek piano. She knew she shouldn't be in the studio, shouldn't be sitting down in front of the keys, but it was like being pulled like a magnet, and Andrea couldn't help herself.

Her fingers pressed down on the keys before she could stop herself and Andrea closed her eyes and let the music warm her soul. She had felt impossibly cold for weeks now and couldn't bring herself to even dream of touching an instrument because it stirred up things she didn't want to think about. She was secure in the knowledge that Declan wouldn't hear her unless he came out of his booth.

Andrea started off by playing a little bit of Clair de lune by Debussy and then shifting into Ed Sheeran's bloodstream. She had heard the mix by a very talented artist called Tokio Myers and loved it, but didn't have all the tools here to do his version justice so she just played the piano and let her fingers soothe her troubled soul.

She didn't realize she had started singing, until she heard her voice in the acoustic of the room, tried to keep her tone low to keep anyone from hearing her because unlike the booth, this space wasn't sound-proof, but Rhys had once said that her voice was something that could not be contained, was not subtle and it matched her personality.

Letting the melody and the song wash over her, Andrea kept her eyes clamped shut, her fingers relying on nothing but memory to hit the right notes, and once the Ed Sheeran version had reached its climax, she switched back to Clair de lune, not wanting to finish the song but knowing that soon, she'd have an audience that she didn't want to explain herself to.

Andrea finished her tinkering with the keys and exhaled, resting her hands on the lid as she opened her eyes and the air was sucked from her lungs.

Declan stood by the door of the studio, his lips

slightly parted, his blue eyes focused on her with an expression on his face that Andrea could only describe as hunger. He licked his lips and took a step toward her, his intentions clear in his eyes even as she stood up, ready to get out of the studio as fast as she could.

But to make a hasty retreat she would have to get passed Declan and her legs, and Christ, her body, didn't want her to go. Her core clenched at the savage intensity in Declan's eyes and she shivered, her brain telling her to get the hell out of dodge but her stupid heart telling her that she had to know what it felt like...even if it was just this once.

Chapter Twenty-Three

Andrea

Declan edged toward her, Andrea taking a shaky step backward, holding up her hands. "Declan, wait."

His growl of frustration felt like a stroke along her body but he halted his pursuit of her. "When I heard someone at the piano, I knew it was you. It felt like with each note, you were calling me to you, like a siren. I watched the look of ecstasy on your face, Andi and yano what I was thinking about?" Declan asked her and when she shook her head, he took a step forward, he gave her a wolfish grin.

"I was wondering if your face would look like that when I made you come."

Andrea bit back a groan, trying to convince her face to give off an emotionless mask, even if she couldn't still the rapid beating of her heart or cool the heat in her veins. Her face felt flush and her breasts felt tight, and her knickers already felt wet and ready for Declan to make her orgasm.

"You can keep wondering, Declan. It's never going to happen."

His lips curved deeper into a smug smirk that plucked on Andrea's temper. She wanted to throw something at him, and she wanted to slap some sense into herself, but she couldn't help but want to feel those talented fingers play her body like the strings of his favourite guitar.

"We've been having this verbal foreplay for years, Andi. *Years.* I've stroked myself to madness, your name a curse on my lips. I had the thought that I was a stupid kid who was too afraid of losing you and that I wasn't your first. Those nights with you on the other side of the wall were slow torture."

Declan took another step toward her and she shook her head, unable to stop herself from wanting him. Andrea tried to convince herself that she could be strong, walk right out that door but inside she knew she couldn't.

"Jesus Christ, Andi...I'm gonna go mad if I don't touch you."

His words seemed to break through the haze of her lust and it gave her a brief moment of clarity. Everything Declan said, it was all about him. He would go mad if he didn't touch her, he was pissed he hadn't been her first but what about *her*? He had slept with a skanky bitch without thinking about what it would do to her and then he had treated her like shit.

It was almost enough to douse the flames of desire kindling inside of her and she found the strength to move, shaking her head with a string of curse words before she headed toward the exit and away from all this insanity.

Declan grabbed her arm, holding her in place, and she snapped her head around to glare at him, trying to let him see the venom in her eyes, and yet, one look into his blue eyes and the heat in them and she knew she was lost.

Andrea wasn't sure who moved first, him, her, or both of them at the same time but then Declan's hands cupped her face, his lips crashing hard against hers and if she thought she was on fire before, it was nothing compared to the inferno that engulfed her now.

What started out as a deceptive crescendo burst into a heart stopping climax as she gave in to her body, parted her lips, and let Declan lap his tongue against hers, his hands in her hair until she struggled to breathe, to think, to comprehend the vicious drumbeat of her heart.

She felt the hardness of him against her stomach, and she couldn't stop the moan that escaped her lips, vibrating the kiss as Declan continued to devour her mouth. Andrea had fantasied about kissing Declan so many times but her mind paled in comparison to this brutal claiming that made her feel like she would explode with one single touch.

Declan broke the kiss and immediately looked deep into her eyes, taking a deep breath before he took her mouth once more, and then she was kissing him back with a fever, tasting and sucking, her eyes closing as she lost herself to madness and didn't care if she ever felt sane again.

Hands blazed a trail down her arms, her waist, then Declan's hands cupped her ass and hoisted her up to sit on the sturdy piano. She wrapped her legs around his waist as Declan slipped his hands under her tee and cupped her breasts, his thumbs pressed hard against her pert nipples.

When Andrea let her head fall back, a moan echoing throughout the room, Declan growled and licked up the curve of her neck before he bit down gently and her entire body jerked, wanting and needing more of what Declan was doing to her.

Reaching down between them, she pulled the strings of his shorts and made to slip her hand into the waistband so she could feel the rigid length of him in the palm of her hand when Declan wrapped his fingers around her wrist.

"Fuck, Andi. Ya, I ...I won't be able to stop if you touch me and I need to lock the door. The guys could walk in any minute and I don't want them to see us."

I don't want them to see us.

It was as if ice-cold water was poured over Andrea and instantly she felt utter shame and horror at what she almost let happen. She had fooled herself that Declan had changed and it was her own fault. Here she was, cut open, body and soul and he still didn't want to be seen with her.

Andrea didn't know an already broken heart could shatter further but here she was bleeding out.

Shoving Declan away from her, his eyes confused as she got down off the piano and righted her clothes, hating the way her eyes teared up. Declan made to reach for her and she flinched, the action making him stop.

"Hey, what happened?"

Andrea wasn't sure if she could verbalize exactly what she wanted to say to him, but the pure look of confusion all over his face only fuelled her anger. She put her hands on his chest and shoved him hard. "How dare you! How fucking dare you!" She was yelling now but Andrea didn't care.

"Is this all a game to you, Declan? Let's toy with Andi and see how much more shit she can take? Is this revenge? Is this punishment for me standing you up? Because if it is, then well done, you've succeeded in killing whatever feelings that I had for you."

Declan's eyes widened for a split second, and Andrea wondered if he even realized what he had said to incite her anger. "Andi, I don't understand. I don't want to hurt you."

"But you keep fucking doing it!" Andrea screamed at him, almost stopping when she saw the members of the band standing outside watching them, horrified expressions on their faces and Rhys looked like he was ready to murder either her or Declan or possibly both of them.

"You keep trying to rip my heart out and stamp on it. I don't want them to see us. That's what you said like I was a dirty secret to be ashamed of. I don't deserve to just be another notch on your bedpost, Declan Walsh. I don't deserve that."

In his defence, Declan looked sick at her words, like he hadn't even considered she would be upset at his words, but here she was, reverting back to seventeen-year-old Andi who had run away from the boy she had loved and five years later, And she was gonna do the same thing again.

Tears cascaded down her cheeks and she let loose a strangled sob before she bolted, running out the door Rhys held open for her and she didn't even stop when Rhys called her name. Andrea was out the door and in her car, reversing out of the space at a speed that would make Charlie proud and as she shifted into first gear, her foot on the accelerator, she glanced in her mirror to see if Declan had come after her.

But Andrea mattered so little to him that Declan couldn't even be bothered to come see if she was okay and he never would. She couldn't do this every day and still remain whole. Andrea had spent her life sorting out everyone else's and now, her own was in tatters and all she wanted to do now was get blind drunk and forget that Declan Walsh ever existed.

She had wanted to come back to Cork with Charlie and start this new chapter of their lives but who the hell was she kidding...there was nothing in Cork for her but heartache and sorrow. Maybe she was better off in Manchester ... Charlie had Noah now and didn't need her as much anymore.

Maybe it was time Andrea Collins took a cold hard look at what she wanted and put the past behind her. Maybe to find any semblance of happiness, she had to forget about what her heart wanted and put Cork in her rear-view mirror.

CHAPTER TWENTY-FOUR

Declan

"You keep trying to rip my heart out and stamp on it. I don't want them to see us. That's what you said like I was a dirty secret to be ashamed of. I don't deserve to just be another notch on your bedpost, Declan Walsh. I don't deserve that."

Declan had spent the last few days trying to call Andi but her phone said it was switched off so he alternated between getting blind ass drunk and leaving her voicenotes. He couldn't get the look on Andi's face out of his mind and he knew he was hurting her.

Rhys had told him as much the moment Andi left the studio, his best friend almost decking him again but Jameson had stepped in to stop Rhys from unleashing his wrath on Declan.

"Just let her go, Deco. Let my sister find someone who doesn't make her think she is unworthy of being loved. You reel her in only to push her away and I can't watch her destroy herself for you. I'll walk away from the band unless you stop."

There had been raised voices then, with everyone screaming at one another until Declan had picked up a guitar and unleashed his anger on the goddamn piano, battering it full-on rockstar style until the wood splintered on both instruments, shards digging into his skin.

That had been a week ago and today was the first day that the band would all be together in the same room. Declan wasn't sure if Rhys would turn up or not, even though Jamie had called him yesterday and told him that Rhys was willing to come if the subject of Andi was off the table.

But Andi was never off the table for him. The kiss played over and over in his mind, it kept him awake and made his body harden. He wanted to seek out Andi and explain that he hadn't meant that he didn't want the band to see them together, he had just wanted to protect her from the guys seeing them fucking on the piano.

He would sing it from the rooftops if she wanted him to prove that he would be fucking proud to have her by his side, as his equal, day after day, night after night. He would do anything to prove to Andi that he didn't mean to hurt her, he just tended to act the fool whenever she was around.

Declan understood why Andi had reacted the way she had and to be fair, his words sounded wrong, especially when he had already hurt her in other ways that would lead her to think the worst of him. Even replaying the words blurted out in a haze of desire and daftness made him shudder.

Trudging down the stairs, Declan ran his fingers through his hair as he made his way into the studio. He heard Rhys's laughter and a feminine chuckle that didn't belong to Luna or Andi. Pushing open the door, Declan frowned when he saw Rhys lounging on one of the chairs, a red-haired woman perched on the arm, her sultry gaze all over Rhys as he grinned at her.

Jameson lifted his head when Declan thundered in, Luna stopped tapping on her drum kit and they all waited to see what Declan did next. He must have looked a state, his hair and beard disheveled and Declan considered he might reek a bit as he hadn't been very hygienic over the last week. Or perhaps it was the bottle of whiskey that dangled from his fingers that gave them cause for concern.

Declan roamed his eyes over the redhead and scowled. Her skirt was so short that Declan no doubt knew that she was flashing Rhys her knickers and her boots were laced up to her knees. She wore a barely-there blouse in the same red as her lipstick.

The woman rose when she noticed Declan come in, glancing down at his bare feet before she flashed him a seductive smile, held out her hand, and said in a British accent. "Nicolette Todd. Rebel PR sent me to go over the details for the collaboration with Oli."

Declan and Oliver Scott had been in contact a few times over the last couple weeks and Declan had asked Oli to drop some vocals on a song and Oli was stoked to do it. Declan thought Andi would be the one to come with the contract but here was this woman standing in his studio who didn't care about music and would sure as shit drop her knickers for any of the band if it thought it would get her some notoriety.

"Where's Andi?" His words came out sounding slurred and that made Jameson get to his feet, standing behind the woman and shaking his head at Declan, who promptly ignored him.

Nicolette smiled and waved a dismissive hand in his direction. "Oh, don't worry. Andi sent me to deal with the band and she may have me handle all things Heartache Melody from now on."

That ignited the anger inside Declan's chest and he snarled. "Where the fuck is Andi?"

The woman took a step back and looked at Rhys or Jameson to help her as she said softly. "Andi wasn't feeling well so she asked me to come. But she has been asked by Joshua James to go with him to America while he shoots a new TV series. She could be gone for over a year so she wanted to see if I would get on with you guys over Shane before she decided who to delegate to."

A year, an entire year before Andi would step foot in Ireland again. Andi was running away from him all over again and he wasn't going to have it. He just wasn't.

Lifting the bottle, Declan took a large slug, the burning like a comfort in the state he was in. "You tell Andi that the deal is over if she doesn't show up. The band works with her and no one else. So, no more recording singles for an album that won't ever come out if she keeps running from me. I'm done. I'm fucking done. There is no point to this if she's not here. The music doesn't feel the same. I'm done."

To punctuate his point, Declan flung the half-empty bottle at the nearest wall, letting it crash and shatter, the liquid pouring down the wall as Nicolette let loose a shriek, gathered up her stuff, and rushed for the door.

When she was gone, Jameson came forward. "Dec, mate. Come on...this isn't you."

Rhys was still lounging on the chair, but his eyes were firmly fixed on Declan. There was a flash of something dark in Rhys's eyes before he shoved off the chair and came at Declan, shoving a finger into his chest but Declan barely felt it, he barely felt anything at all.

"You're a selfish prick, Declan. Andi has made her decision and you need to let her go. Let her go and be happy and find someone who will love her."

Declan grabbed Rhys by the collar of his leather jacket. "I fucking love her."

Rhys barked out a laugh, rolling her eyes. "Do you? Then you have a funny way of showing it. If you care about her like you say you do, let my sister go. You don't deserve her."

Declan pushed Rhys away with a snarl so he wouldn't give in to the urge to strangle him. He looked around at the faces of his bandmates, his friends, and couldn't stand the pity in their eyes.

"Get out the lot of you. Leave me the fuck alone."

Rhys snorted, heading for the door before he turned and smirked. "You lecture me on public image but here you are, willing to throw away the band's chances of making it because of your wounded pride. I'm glad she overheard you telling me that you weren't interested. Stop playing the fucking victim and sort your shit out. Just leave my sister alone."

Declan lunged for Rhys, and felt Jameson drag him back before Rhys disappeared from view, Luna following out after Rhys with a sadness that echoed his own. Jameson let him go and faced him. "Rhys is right, Dec. You gotta sort yourself out. You might be the singer but you aren't the whole band. You can't rip away our dreams because you bruised your heart. Don't do this to us."

Staring after Jameson long after he left, Declan didn't know what to do to make right all the wrongs in his life. He continued to fuck up with Andi anytime he opened his mouth to speak but, music and lyrics never failed him. He could prove to everyone that Andi needed to be with him and he needed her more than anything else in his life.

So he grabbed a pen and a pad, sat down right there on the floor, and poured his heart out into a song, written just for Andi, and hours maybe days later when he finished, he picked up the phone and called Jameson.

"Jay, get the band together mate. I need your help."

CHAPTER TWENTY-FIVE

Andrea

WEEKS HAD PASSED since the disastrous kiss in the studio and Andrea had to comfort Nicolette who came to Andrea in tears because Declan had frightened her. The fact that Declan had been violent had surprised her because the man she knew had never had that streak in him; he might be an ass with the ability to cut with his words, but Declan couldn't hurt anyone physically.

Even if he had damaged her irrevocably with words.

Andrea had kept herself busy, making plans with Charlie for the office in Cork, dealing with a few loose ends in Manchester, but it wasn't until the end of their zoom call, after a shirtless Noah had come to kiss Charlie on the cheek before heading for a run with Quinn, that Charlie had brought up Declan.

"I don't know how to phrase this without adding to your pain but have you decided on what you want to do about the Heartache Melody contract?"

Andrea sighed and shook her head. "Not really. Part of me has all of these ideas and plans for the band and it'd kill me not to push forward with them, but I don't know if I can mentally take any more where he's concerned."

Charlie fiddled with her engagement ring absent-mindedly, and Andrea was sure her friend didn't realize she was doing it. "JJ told me about America."

JJ had asked her to come to the US with him while he went to shoot the new tv show for a streaming service, and Andrea would be lying if she said she wasn't tempted. A year spent living in LA with JJ, building up her client base while she soaked up the sunshine seemed like just the right kind of medicine for her right now but there was a Declan sized weight stopping her from saying yes.

"Noah and I argued last night over you two."

Arching her brows at her friend in question, Charlie waved her hand and chuckled. "Don't worry, we had lots of make-up sex after."

"TMI, Charlie...TMI."

Charlie laughed as she glanced over her shoulder like she expected Noah to come back in and disturb them. "Noah said that Declan looked wrecked. He was arguing that he was in Declan's position once and someone with a backbone of steel told him that when two people look at each other like you two do, it can only end in love or hate. He really didn't want it to end in hate for the both of ye."

Andrea was surprised that Noah had remembered their little conversation and even more so that he had told Charlie. It had worked out for Charlie and Noah, though not without a few bumps along the way, but the odds of it happening for her and Declan as well didn't look great.

"I told him that things were different for you guys and to just let you sort it out for yourselves. Noah's response was if no one had interfered with the two of us, then we might not be engaged, or even together, and you and Declan were a hundred times more stubborn than us."

That made Andrea laugh, because it was true. She was well known for her stubborn streak as was Declan. But she wasn't ready to come to a conclusion just yet on if she would take JJ up on his offer, or would just admit to being a masochist and continue to work with the band no matter how much pain it caused her.

Andrea was invested in the success of the band, in her brother's success so there was no right way to go about making her decision. At least JJ had told her to take all the time she needed to make up her mind so she didn't have to make a hasty decision.

Her phone rang then and she glanced at it, having had the phone on do not disturb for over a week after she said goodbye to Charlie and braced herself for the sound of Declan's voice on the other end of the private number calling her.

"Andrea Collins."

"Andrea, hi, this is Cindy Maher calling. I hope you don't mind but Oli Scott gave me your number." The woman went on to tell Andrea that she was calling from a well-known radio station that had a section on the show where bands and artists came in to do a live session and then covered a popular song. Andrea's throat went dry and her pulse quickened because if Cindy was calling about what she thought she was, this could be huge for the band.

"I was chatting to Oli and he was telling me all about this epically talented band from Ireland who had invited him to appear on their debut album and that I should know all about them. Oli normally only likes to blow his own trumpet so I looked the band up. I agree that they are stars in the making."

Andrea took a minute before she responded. "They are. It's been a while since a band came from Ireland and could rival the likes of Inhaler, and The Blizzards, and The Coronas. Plus, they are Cork-born and bred so I had to get behind them, even if the keyboard player is my little brother."

That made Cindy laugh and they spoke at great length about the members of the band, with Cindy telling Andrea that Oli had been quite taken with Luna's talent on the drums. Cindy offered her hope that Luna's twin would be okay and then she said the words Andrea was waiting to hear.

"We had a band pull out of a performance next week and would love to get the band on the airwaves. I've taken the liberty to book you all into a hotel nearby so all I need now is a yes and we can start advertising the band for next week."

It was an easy yes for Andrea as her excitement grew and she thanked Cindy for the call and she would see her in London next week. The moment the phone call ended, Andrea jumped up from her chair and let out a whoop of delight, then shot Oli a text to thank him for opening the door for the band.

The first person she wanted to call was Declan, but Andrea was not prepared for how that conversation would start and she was too excited to let Declan drag down her mood. After talking to her brother earlier this morning, Andrea knew the band had been holed up in the studio working on songs so she dialed her brother's number.

"Andi, hey...I'm with the band so can call you back later."

She ignored Rhys's worried tone and told him it was okay and she needed to talk to the entire band so would Rhys mind putting her on speaker.

"Andi, you're on speaker now."

For a moment, Andi didn't know if she could get

the words out but then she heard Declan clear his throat as if he meant to say something so she just blurted out the news. "You guys need to get spruced up and to London. I don't know how he managed it but you lot owe Oli a keg of beer because I have just got off the phone with Cindy Maher who said Oli was singing all your praises."

Andrea went on to explain that they would be on the biggest radio station in the UK next week and on one of the most listened to shows. Then the band were cheering and shouting and Andrea was laughing along with them.

She felt their elation and was thrilled to be a little part of it, even if it was just a small sliver of it. The idiots on the other end of the phone started to sing *Ole Ole*, like they were at a football game and Andrea rolled her eyes.

"Andi? You still there?"

Andrea drowned out the din going on as the phone went off speaker, "Ya, I am."

Suddenly, there was a snick of a door and a gaping silence as she waited to hear Declan speak and when he did, it felt like being punched. "You'll be there next week, right?"

Cindy had said she wanted to see Andrea and yet, she hoped to avoid a face-to-face where Declan would open his mouth and his beautiful voice would make her forget all that had happened between them.

But she also knew Declan would dig his heels in

and this was too big of a deal to watch fall apart because she was afraid to see him again. This was the dream they had whispered about, nights sat under the stars that were easier than painful conversations over the phone.

She would go to the radio show and she would see if she could survive the onslaught and that would make the decision for her there and then. She should stay or should she take JJ up on his offer.

One way or another, next week would decide her future.

"I'll be there, Declan. I'll be there."

CHAPTER TWENTY-SIX

Andrea

ANDREA HAD ARRIVED in London the night before, checking into the hotel and letting Rhys drag her out to dinner with Jameson. They didn't mention their bandmate and Andrea was grateful for the reprieve. Rhys was taking it easier than he normally did, which was a shock to Andrea but she didn't mention it.

When a group of Irish girls spotted them, Rhys was more than happy to pose for pictures while Jameson didn't seem all that comfortable with the attention, frowning when Andrea told him to get used to it, because, after tomorrow, there was no going back.

Jameson went off to answer a phone call and then he came back to the table, tossed some money onto it, and left, a grim expression on his face. After Rhys was done taking selfies, they walked the short distance back to the hotel where Andrea saw a figure leaning over the wall by the river and she unlinked her arm from Rhys.

"I'll see you tomorrow." She told him, surprised when Rhys blocked her way.

"Be sure, Andi, be sure before you pull the pin on the grenade and we can't get back from you and him."

Andrea opened her mouth to respond but Rhys was already heading into the hotel as she looked over to where Declan leaned, looking out at the water. She knew he couldn't sleep the night before a performance, at least not when she knew him back then and even when it was a stupid school play that he was singing in, Declan had nerves that betrayed his cool and calm exterior.

Her trainers made no sound as she came to stand beside Declan, leaning over the wall and gazing into the murky water to avoid looking directly at him. "Not thinking of jumping, are ya?"

Declan chuckled softly, glancing at her before he looked back at the water. "Nah. Water looks cold. Just bracing myself in case you wanted to chuck me in."

"Tempting as that might be, I need you to be able to sing tomorrow. Otherwise..." Andrea let her voice trail off and then she shrugged, causing Declan to bark out a laugh and she watched some of the tension leave his shoulders.

They stayed standing side by side, their elbows

almost touching for a while, and then Declan grew restless like he had too much energy to burn. He kept sneaking glances at her, as if he wanted to say something but was afraid of saying something stupid again.

"Hey, you wanna take a walk? I could do with working off the dinner Rhys and Jameson all but shoved down my throat. I feel like it put on a stone in weight or maybe that was the sundae I pigged out on."

"You don't need to ever worry 'bout your weight, Andi. You always look damn sexy to me."

Andrea flushed, pushing off the wall and striding down along the riverfront, Declan falling into step with her, his long lazy strides powerful. They didn't say anything, just walked and when Andrea shivered, Declan removed his hoody and draped it over her shoulders, and Andreas almost forgot why there was this awkwardness between them.

Almost.

"Are you nervous about tomorrow?" Andrea asked, slipping her hands into the arms of Declan's hoody and rolling up the sleeves because it was miles too big for her.

"I've been dreaming for the last week that when I open my mouth to sing, it just comes out in German like I'm taking part in Eurovision or some shit."

Andrea narrowed her eyes. "But you don't speak German."

"I think that's the crazy part. I have no clue what I'm singing."

Laughing out loud, Andrea shook her head. "You'll be grand. And sure, if you feel yourself getting nervous, just close your eyes and pretend there's no one else in the room. Just you and the music. There's no one listening to you but the empty room, and everything will be okay."

"I do that but when I close my eyes, I imagine it's you standing there and the nerves just go away. I think I could die a happy man if I could just spend my life singing to you and no one else."

She didn't know how to respond to that, so she just smiled and changed the subject, asking if Luna would be okay. "I told the presenter that any questions about Luke were off-limits and the moment someone had the audacity to bring him up, I'd cut them off. Same with Jamie's past. Tomorrow is about the music and not the gossip pages."

Declan skidded to a halt and turned to face her, Andrea tilting her head up to look into his bright blue eyes. He tentatively reached out, running his hands up her arms.

"You always have the band's best intentions at heart, dontcha. That's why you have to stay and manage us, stay and be part of this journey with us, with me. Don't leave us, Andi, don't leave me."

Andrea was shocked at the way his voice broke at the end of his sentence, even more so when he leaned down and pressed his lips to hers for the briefest of moments before he took a step back, turned, and walked back the way they had come, pausing to glance over his shoulder and wait for her.

Her mind was a jumble, unable to process the most civil conversation they'd had in years and the softness of the kiss that happened so quickly, she wasn't sure if she had imagined it. When she lifted her fingers to her mouth and saw the slight smile on Declan's lips, she knew it had happened, but she wasn't sure how she felt about it.

"Me mam made sure the boys all knew to tune in tomorrow. She had invited the entire street over to tune in, and has warned me to make sure that we don't let the family down by singing something lewd or swearing. I told her that it was Rhys and Luna she needed to talk to 'cause I was an angel and never fucking swore."

Andrea snorted and rolled her eyes. "Dream on, Dec, dream on. Wait until you have to do magazine covers and do all rockstar sexy poses that will leave your ma's bingo club reaching for their hot flush medication. You'll have an army of cougars after you."

Declan barked out a laugh. "You'll protect me from the cougars, right?"

Andrea gave him a little noncommittal shrug of her shoulders. "I'm not sure. I don't think that's in my contract. I'm only responsible for getting you the covers. Fighting off the bingo squad will cost ya extra. Maybe you could deflect them towards Rhys?"

Declan grinned at her then and it was like the years

had slipped away and they were bantering with one another like old times, before they had fallen apart, and she had done a runner. Andrea took in his eyes, the slant of his mouth, the way his stubble framed those full lips and it made her stagger, with Declan reaching out to steady her.

"I got you. I'll always be there to stop you from falling."

Her heart skipped a beat as she tried to brush it off, glancing at the river before she responded. "You just want to make sure I don't toss you into the river."

Andrea swore she saw his smile falter, then he winked. "Sure, that's it. And to protect me from cougars."

She couldn't help but return his smile, then she yawned and clapped a hand over her mouth, offering an apology but Declan just rested his hand on the small of her back, leading her inside the hotel and toward the elevator. He pressed the button, seemingly unaware that there was a photographer standing to the side, his camera phone out as Declan reached out and tucked a strand of hair behind her ear, then grazed his lips across her cheek.

"Good night, Andrea."

"Good night, Declan." Her tone came out huskier than she wanted and his eyes flared before he took a step back, and walked to the stairwell, leaving her to lean against the wall and let out a harsh curse before she slipped into the elevator, thankful she was on a different floor to the band.

Andrea wasn't sure what she had expected to happen when she went to talk to Declan tonight, but it wasn't the easy banter and chaste kisses they had shared. It left her even more confused than she had been and now, she wasn't sure what to feel.

Perhaps Declan had ruined her for anyone else. She had known the intensity of his kiss; had felt the way his hands had moved over her body and she hated herself that she still wanted more. Andrea still wanted the picture in her head of a happily ever after with Declan. She wanted him to steal kisses when he left her like Noah did with Charlie and for everyone to know that they were a thing.

Tomorrow would be the start of Declan's step into stardom and once he was centre stage, he would forget all about her and what might have been.

CHAPTER TWENTY-SEVEN

Declan

THE FIRST PART of the radio show had gone off without a hitch, with the band answering some general questions about how the band got together and what made them work so well together. Declan had explained that they were more than just a band, that they were a family and the bonds of friendship ran deep. He told the presenter that there was no frontman in the band, that they were all equal members, he just happened to have the best voice.

That had made everyone laugh and Declan kept glancing toward where Andi was standing on the other side of the glass, watching them. Someone said something to her and she grinned, nodding her head and the presenter started speaking again.

"And I believe that you also recently made a friend with everyone's favourite rogue, Oli Scott. So much so that he's announced Heartache Melody as his main support on tour later this year."

"Oli's been great and his writing process is amazing to see. I hope he doesn't mind me saying but we are working on a track for the album and that track is gonna be kickass to play on tour."

They chatted away about music for a while and then the presenter glanced over her shoulder and Andi flashed her a grin and a thumbs up.

"The entire country is wondering what you guys are doing for the August bank holiday?"

Declan hadn't a clue what she was on about but Rhys grinned. "That depends if it's the Irish bank holiday or the English one?"

The entire studio seemed to descend into silence as the presenter continued. "How would you fancy head-lining the introducing stage at the Reading and Leeds festival?"

Declan felt like he had been hot by a two-by-four and was rendered speechless. There was a chorus of hell yeahs, and let's go before they cut to commercial and they set up to perform.

"Did you know about Reading and Leeds?" He asked Rhys as he pulled the strap of his guitar over his head.

"Andi told me not to say anything until it was official. She only got the invite this morning. I can't bloody wait. You sure you wanna do this song today?"

He glanced over his shoulder at Andi, then back to Rhys. "Ya, let's go. Go big or go home, guys."

Rhys bumped his fist against Declan's before shrugging off his jacket and getting behind his keyboard. Jameson settled into his position, while Luna pulled back her hair off her face and flashed him the biggest smile he'd seen on her in weeks.

They got the countdown that they were going live again and the presenter introduced them. "If you are just joining us, you are about to hear something special from the band we just announced as headliners for the introducing stage at Reading and Leeds this year. Turn up your radios and prepare to be blown away. Over to you Declan."

His heart felt like it was lodged in his throat as he opened his mouth. "Thanks for having us, folks, we are Heartache Melody and this is a song we only finished last week but will be the first single from our self-titled album. It's called Rebel Heart and it's a song about the girl who got away and still being in love with her even after all this time."

He lifted his gaze to where Andi was standing, a hand over her mouth as he counted down from three to one and they let Luna have her moment. She pounded on the drums with a vicious beat that had his head moving and after her solo ended, Rhys joined in on the keyboard and soon after, he and Jameson let their fingers strike the strings and the song came together.

Now he just had to sing his heart out and make sure that Andi heard the sincerity in his voice.

"Nights spent under the stars,
I still only had eyes for you.
The girl with the rebel heart
And a fast pair of running shoes."

Andi's eyes widened, one hand still over her mouth and the other over her heart. His fingers fumbled over the strings and he slammed his eyes shut, swinging the guitar to his back and he just took the mic and poured all his pain, his guilt into the lyrics.

"I wish we could go back,
To when I didn't make you cry,
When I almost got to call you mine,
Nights spent under darkened skies.
We got lost in lyrics and melody,
I got lost in your infectious smile,
Then I went and messed it up
And you ran a mile"

Luna came back in then, with a savage beat, the drums pounding hard and fast as Declan sang the chorus.

"I'm still in love with the girl
With a rebel heart,
I'm in love with a girl.
Whose love I tore apart."

Then Luna's fierce drumbeat stopped with Jamie and Rhys playing off one another. Luna tapped her drumsticks against the cymbal and Declan turned away from the microphone to beat his fist against the snare before Luna swatted him away with a laugh as Rhys danced his fingers over the keys and then Declan went back to singing.

"I close my eyes and all I see is you,
Your kiss is tattooed on my brain,
You're standing right there and
It's driving me insane.
I'm still in love with the girl
With a rebel heart,
I'm in love with a girl.
Whose love I tore apart.
All the songs that I sing
were written just for you,
So, I could tell the world about
the girl with the rebel heart."

The hard rock of the melody ground to a halt as Rhys switched to a more classical tone, one that Declan knew Andi would understand was solely in reference to her, as Declan tried to soften the gruff tone of his voice.

"You were looking at the world,
But I only had eyes for you,
Waiting for you to notice me,
Falling in love with you."

Luna tapped her drums with her sticks again

counting in for them to rock out once more and Declan pulled his guitar back to the front and he and Jameson jammed together for a couple of bars, then they both leaned into the mic to sing.

"I'm still in love with the girl

With a rebel heart,

I'm in love with a girl.

Whose love I tore apart."

Then the melody died down to a hush, with Declan playing the last few chords, his eyes opening slowly to look out into the viewing area, Andi's eyes on him in utter disbelief as Declan played the last few chords by himself and he looked her dead in the eye as he sang the last verse of the song solo.

"Cause I'm still in love

With the girl with the rebel heart

You were looking at the world,

But I only had eyes for you."

Claps rang out throughout the studio when they finished and Declan felt elated as he looked over to where Andi had been standing just to see her walk out the door and his heart sank further than it had ever sunk before.

But he faked a grin and chatted away with the presenter before it was time for them to do their cover song. It hadn't been easy picking the song but they had thrown all the options into a hat and in the end, it was Luna's choice that was chosen and Declan just had to sing Paramore's *The Only Exception,* the words cutting him with every word he sang as all he wanted to do was to chase after Andi.

He went through the motions and the show ended, and Declan and the band were left alone for a few minutes as Luna came up and threw her arms around him. "Oh, Dec. I'm sorry. I can't believe Andi just walked out."

"Are you gonna just let her walk away, again?" Rhys demanded from behind his keyboard.

"I think your sister made her decision. I laid it all out and she still fucking ran."

"You ever think maybe she wants you to run after her? For a smart man, you can be a fuckin' idiot sometimes."

Declan was quiet all the way back to the hotel, even though he should be walking on air right now. All the band's dreams were coming true and they were finally exactly where they had wanted to be but he couldn't help the morose feeling in his chest.

Maybe this was what he deserved after everything, to finally be upfront about his feelings for Andi, and after last night, he had sensed a shift between them, that gave him hope, for it to be ripped away in a public way and now every time he sang the word to Rebel Heart, it would be a gut punch.

Karma had found her way to swing back around and she really was a bitch.

Chapter Twenty-Eight

Andrea

"*Cause I'm still in love*
  With the girl with the rebel heart
  You were looking at the world,
  But I only had eyes for you."

Anger had bled into her veins the moment she had realized that Declan had chosen such a public way of expressing his feelings. And of course, she had been in utter shock from the intro to the lyrics belted out by the rock god himself. How dare he claim to be in love with her when he had treated her so badly, and then he had the nerve to profess his love live on the radio. It had been too much for her to comprehend.

When the final chords of the music began to play,

Andrea had bolted and not looked back, because she knew if Declan looked at her that she would toss everything aside and give in to the part of her heart that was telling her to let herself fall for Declan.

But hadn't she always been in love with him?

Hours later, back at the hotel, Andrea paced her hotel room, the anger in her chest as painful as the ache of her broken heart. Her phone rang and when she saw Charlie's name on it, she silenced the call before she could stop herself, Andrea tossed the phone on the bed and stormed down the hall and into the elevator.

Seconds later, she stood outside Declan's hotel room, her fist raised as she pounded on the door hard and kept knocking until a nearly naked Declan opened the door, a towel wrapped around his waist and a bottle of whiskey in his hands.

He looked ...broken...his eyes narrowing as if he didn't believe that she was standing right there in front of him. Her eyes scanned over the broad shoulders, and the corded muscles on his abdomen, and traced the dark dusting of hair that ran from his navel and disappeared under the towel.

Andrea's mouth was suddenly dry and for a moment she forgot why exactly she was there until she dragged her gaze from his magnificent body and beheld the beginning of a smug smile on his lips.

"You asshole!" she snarled, shoving him hard so that he took a step back into the hotel room. Andrea followed after him, letting the door slam shut as she jabbed a finger into his chest. "How dare you pretend to care about me to write some song. How dare you use it to vilify me and make the entire world think that the fucking girl you were singing about broke *your* heart."

"I didn't use you, Andi. Every time I open my damn mouth to speak, I end up saying stupid shit. I get tongue-tied around you and this song, it was my way of apologizing for what I said, what I did, and to be honest with you about how I feel about you. How I've always felt about you."

Her heart lurched at his words and she stopped. Then realized that they stood not even an arm's length away from one another. Declan's eyes looked defeated, like he fully expected her to turn on her heels and run away again. Her entire body thrummed with a new sensation and wetness pooled at her core.

Before she could constrain herself, before she could let logic rule over her heart and consider just how colossal a mistake her next actions could lead to, Andrea closed the distance between them and, hooking her hands around Declan's neck, dragged his lips down to hers and kissed him.

Declan responded immediately, dropping the whiskey bottle to the floor, then his hands in her hair as he tilted her head to deepen the kiss, waking them backward, her back slamming into the wall as Declan pressed his body against hers, the evidence of his arousal hard against her stomach. He kissed her like he needed the air in her lungs to breathe and he kept kissing her until they both broke apart struggling to breathe.

It's just one night...just one night...

That was what she told herself as Declan leaned in to kiss her jaw, her throat, all while his fingers rubbed against her core and she let loose a throaty moan, throwing her head back as Declan continued to rub his fingers back and forth over her leggings and it made her arch her hips toward him.

Declan didn't say anything as she looked up at him, his face determined as he kissed her again. Andrea roamed her hands down his bare chest, dragging her nails over his hard nipples and she almost came when the vibration of his growl went all the way down to where his fingers were.

Andrea needed more, so she pushed him back just long enough to yank off her leggings and pulled her hoody off, then quickly divested herself of her thong and bra. She felt like a goddess as Declan's eyes devoured her body and he licked his lips.

Andrea made to stride forward, to rip the towel from his waist and get him inside her before either of them could change their mind. But it seemed Declan had other ideas.

He palmed her breasts as he walked her back against the wall, using his big thigh to push her legs apart, and dropped to his knees. Andrea sucked in a breath as his fingers played in the curls just above where she needed his fingers, his tongue, and her hands went into his hair the moment he sank a finger inside her and her knees felt like jelly, heat spreading over her entire body as Declan grinned up at her, then ducked his head to flick his tongue over her already drenched core.

"Fuck, Declan." Her nails scraped against his scalp and she was about to urge him to continue, the tingling building inside her that told her climax was close but Declan seemed to know already when she wanted and needed as he latched his mouth to her core and sucked, licked and plunged his tongue in and out of her folds, alternating between his fingers and his tongue, mimicking sex until the pressure built and built, Declan's free hand clamped on her right thigh to stop her from falling even as her orgasm hit her hard and she screamed his name, her body jerking towards his as he used his talented fingers to ease her down from coming apart.

Then Declan was in front of her, kissing her, his tongue plundering her mouth as it had her sex and she tasted herself on his tongue. And then they were moving, toward the bed and Andrea scooted backward on the bed as Declan dropped the towel and his cock stood long and proud, as she made to reach out and stroke the most intimate part of him but Declan was already sheathing his cock in a condom before he pushed apart her thighs and settled himself at her core.

Declan paused at her entrance, leaning down to place his forehead against hers. "Gods, I love you, Andi. I've dreamed of this for bloody years and now that I have you, I don't intend to let you go."

Andrea opened her mouth to tell him that what was happening between them was just for one night, so they could get this out of their system and go their separate ways but even before Declan claimed her body, he had already claimed her heart and she knew that once they were one and done, she would be ruined for anyone else who tried to love her.

Declan kissed her then, stealing the air from her lungs as he rocked his hips, the tip of his erection pushing in before he pulled out, each roll of his hips pushing inside her, inch by blistering inch, the fullness of him filling her, on the edge of pleasure and pain, her walls clenching around him.

Sweat beaded on his forehead as if Declan was holding himself back, his mouth moved to her throat as she felt his body tremble as she ran her hands down his spine, up into his hair as she pulled his gaze toward her. "Give me all of you, Declan. I'm so close again. I need you to move now."

She dragged his lips down to hers, lifting her hips off the bed in order to try and deepen the penetration. Andrea bit down on his bottom lip and that seemed to snap Declan's control.

His cock slid fully inside her and she tore her lips away from his to moan his name. Declan growled, lowering his face to the curve of her neck as he pounded in and out of her, branding her from the inside out as Andrea came hard, her nails scoring his back and she felt Declan's body tense before he shuddered, finding his own release.

They both stayed silent, not wanting to break the spell as Declan brushed her hair from her face and kissed her hard, his cock buried deep inside her still, the weight of his body pressed against hers as he leaned in and whispered. "I love you, Andi."

The words she longed to say caught in her throat as she closed her eyes and feigned falling asleep, waiting until after Declan had disposed of the condom and had fallen asleep beside her before she went to the bathroom to pee and then left a sleeping Declan alone as she ran away once more.

CHAPTER TWENTY-NINE

Declan

ANDI HAD BEEN GONE when he woke the next morning, blissfully content until he realized that the other side of the bed had long since been cold, her scent still lingering in the room as he went to shower and pack, knowing they were heading back to Ireland later in the day after a quick press conference this morning.

He had barely stepped out of the shower and gotten dressed when a knock sounded on his door and his heart pounded in the hopes that it was Andi, and not Jameson who actually stood at the door, a coffee in each hand.

"I thought you might need a coffee after the sex

gymnastics I heard last night." his friend teased, then glanced around the room. "Where's Andi?"

Declan took the coffee from Jameson and shook his head. "She left."

"Ah Dec, mate, I'm sorry."

That was all that Jameson had said, letting him wallow in his broken heart even at the press conference, where Declan had been hoping to see Andi, but she hadn't turned up. Instead, he stared blankly at the exit as reporters tossed questions at the band.

"Declan, Declan! Tell us more about the mysterious Rebel Heart girl!"

Normally, Declan wouldn't have bothered answering those kinda questions, but at this point, if he had already lost Andi, then he couldn't lose her more, could he?

"Let me tell you a little about the Rebel Heart girl," He began, his tone sounding like he'd been on the drink for a week straight, his bandmates looking at him with wide eyes. "I've been in love with her since I was seventeen and too stupid to realize that the woman I wanted to marry was right there beside me. I messed up and now, maybe too much time has passed between us, too many angry words and hurt feelings. But I still love her and I always will."

Declan shifted his gaze to the camera and he looked into it as if there was not a gazillion lights and faces watching him, and that he could just be looking into Andi's eyes and putting his heart on display for her.

"I'm sorry I was a fool. I'm sorry I pushed you away, and I'm sorry for not telling you that I loved you sooner. I always say the wrong thing around you because you tie me in knots but I need the world to know that I am so in love with you, Andrea Collins. And I will still be in love with you until the air leaves my lungs and my heart stops beating."

Declan rose from his seat and headed for the door, the band following out after him. Declan didn't say a word on the entire flight, ignoring the band's concerned looks as they dropped him off at home and Jameson told him that he would check in tomorrow.

"Rhys?" Declan as he jumped out of the minibus and held the door open. "Will you just tell me if she's okay? Just text me that she's okay and I'll never ask you for anything again."

Declan closed the door before Rhys could answer and headed inside, going on full alert when he realized the studio door was slightly ajar. He picked up a hurley that was at the bottom of the stairs leading up to his apartment, dropped his holdall, and crept inside.

There was no one in the main communal area but he heard noises coming from the recording studio. His heart kicked like a snare drum as Declan shoved open the doors and he almost dropped the stick from his grasp as Andi looked up from where she was sat behind his piano and offered him a small smile.

"I would be intimidated by the hurley if I didn't know just how shite you were with it."

Declan, despite himself, barked out a laugh and put his weapon of choice away. "What are you doing here, Andi?"

Andi chewed on her bottom lip before she got to her feet, her fingers grazing the keys of the piano before she picked up a wrapped present that sat on top of the piano, striding over to him and holding it out.

"I got you a present," Andi said, her tone husky as she cleared it and then tried again. "Can you open it, please?"

"It's not going to explode or anything is it?" Declan himself tried to use humour to deflect from the tension in the air but all Andi did was smile and shake her head.

Declan ripped open the wrapping and frowned at the box in his hand before he opened the lid to reveal a pair of well-worn purple Nike trainers. Lifting his puzzled gaze, he beheld Andi with her arms around her waist, cheeks flushed.

"I saw you on the news. I heard you when Rhys sent me a voice note of conversations you had when writing the song. I listen to Noah when he called me and ripped me a new one for being just as pigheaded as he was and focusing on the bad."

Declan didn't know what to say, but his hands trembled as Andi took the box and place it back on the piano. "I'm sorry I ran away last night but I was terrified of what could go wrong." She inclined her head to the shoes. "I'm tired of running away, Declan. I'm tired of stressing that we are making the biggest mistake of our lives by trying. I don't want to run anymore so I am giving you my running shoes and my heart."

Declan felt his mouth gape open as Andi blew out a breath. "I love you too, Declan. I always have. I can't say I might not try to run again if I get overwhelmed but I want to try and see if this thing between us is real. So, here I am, Declan, telling you the words I wanted to when I was seventeen but never got the chance. I love you."

Her eyes brimmed with tears, as if she expected him to push her away but Declan closed the distance between them and tugged her into his arms, feeling his heart soar when Andi wrapped her arms around his back and he felt the wetness of her tears soak into his tee.

Declan reluctantly untangled himself from Andi to cup her cheek. "Hey, no tears. I love you. I'm sorry for being a dickhead and I'm sorry for the years that we danced around one another. If you want to go to the US with JJ, we can work it out. But I am never letting you go again, Andi. Not until my heart stops beating."

Andi swiped at her eyes. "I told JJ no. I couldn't leave even if we decided not to try. LA might have been exciting, but the reason me and Charlie wanted to set up Rebel PR in Cork was because we both wanted to come home. Ireland is where we belong."

Declan kissed her then hard, felt her smile into the kiss, and then they were tugging off each other's clothes barely making it to the floor before Declan was thrusting inside of her, each of them declaring their love in the way their hands touched one another and after their climax, they lay on the floor of the studio, Andi draped over his body and Declan knew if he died today, he would die a happy man.

"Move in with me." He blurted out into the quiet, knowing he was probably steamrolling ahead but he didn't care. They had wasted so much time; he didn't want to waste any more of it. "And before you argue, you still haven't found a place and we can redecorate if you want. Plus, I'm hoping the lure of the studio will convince you even if you aren't tempted by the thought of waking up beside me every day. I don't want any walls between us anymore, Andi."

She sucked in a breath as she lifted her head to look at him, then grinned. "Okay, but just so you know...you had me at studio."

They laughed and kissed some more and Declan had to pinch himself that this was real and not all a dream, telling Andi that he hoped she would come along when they travelled the world to tour with Oli.

"I wanna see the world with you, Andi, and then come home with you. I wanna go to sleep beside you every night and wake with you in my arms. And if you want to run, I'll run with you. and if I act the idiot, feel free to call me on it...then we can have lots of makeup sex!"

Andi swatted at his chest as she laughed then got a mischievous gleam in her eyes as she traced her hands across his chest. "How soundproof is this room?"

She didn't give him a chance to respond as she slid down his body, and stroked the length of his cock before she grinned flicked her tongue over the head before taking him into her hot wet mouth and any coherent thoughts fled.

CHAPTER THIRTY

Andrea

ALTHOUGH SHE AND Declan had spent a few weeks mostly horizontal, Andrea kept waiting for the shoe to drop and for a wrongness to settle in once they emerged into the real world. And when it didn't, Andrea hadn't known what to do. They'd been a couple for months now and everything was going as well as it could.

Rhys was the only one struggling to deal with the fact his best friend and his sister were now a couple and kept himself away from any situation that wasn't band-related. Every time Andrea tried to talk to him, Rhys had blown her off and asked her to give him space to make sense of it. And so, she did, confused still because

Declan told her that Rhys had been pushing him to be upfront with her and now, now Rhys could barely stand to be in the same room as them.

Andrea pushed the pain down, knowing she would deal with her brother in time but today was all about the band and her gorgeous rock god as they got to play the Reading and Leeds festival. The band were hyped and lots of family and friends were there to help them celebrate. Andrea stood off to the side of the stage as the band tuned their instruments, with Charlie and Noah keeping her company.

Despite the rocky start she and Noah had gotten off to, he was actually much less of a tight ass than she thought and he could banter as good as she could. Charlie too seemed to be blissfully happy that her fiancé and her best friend were getting on.

"She's missing Luke being here," Noah said suddenly, inclining his head to where Luna had her eyes closed, her hands resting on the necklace of music notes that Luke had bought her for their twenty-first birthday. Noah kissed Charlie's cheek, then strode over and had a few words with Luna, then hugged her as the girl shed a few tears before she composed herself and Noah left her to get in the zone.

"You know, I was wrong about him. He's got a kind heart underneath all the boy racerness."

Charlie laughed and linked her arm with Andrea's. "I could say the same for the rock god. if you had told me a year ago that we would be back in Ireland, both of us with the boys who we loved, I would have laughed at you. but I wouldn't change anything, Andi. If Noah hadn't of broken my heart and Declan hadn't been an utter fool, then we might never have crossed paths and I'd never have found my soul sister."

A lump appeared in Andrea's throat as her eyes blurred. "Fuckin hell, Charlie, you're gonna have me bawling." Then she nudged her friend's shoulder as Noah came back with bottles of water for them all and told them Luna was okay, she just needed a minute to remember that Luke was here with her even if he wasn't physically.

The band had a rapturous set, made even more so when Oli Scott strode out with a cockiness that made Andrea grin, her old friend's public persona making him a lot of money even if she knew that deep down, he was a gentle soul, but as the band rocked out to Never Back Down and Oli unleashed his trademark scream, the crowd lost it and from the reaction, you would swear that the band were headliners.

Oli fist-bumped the band, bowing and raising his middle fingers to the sky before he exited to get ready for his own headline set later in the evening, and in the blink of an eye, Heartache Melody finished their set and Declan all but rushed off stage to take her in his arms and kiss her heard, sweating like a maniac.

The band went off to have their after-performance ritual and although Declan invited her, she left them to it because as much of a part of Declan and Rhys's life that she was, this was their moment and theirs alone, and from the way Declan looked at her, they would have plenty of time to celebrate the first steps at Heartache Melody taking over the world.

Noah and Charlie, along with Declan's brothers kept her company until the band rejoined them and they went to watch Oli's set from the VIP area. Night had fallen around them as the lights dipped, they flared as Oli strutted across the stage like a prince of night, egging the crowd on with the playful wriggle of his fingers, and then he screamed, "Fuck," into the microphone and the pit came alive.

Her feet ached from all the standing and dancing until Oli hushed the crowd. "This song goes out to my friends in Heartache Melody who absolutely killed it today and I can't wait to have them on my new tour. I'm going to Ireland next month to work on me new album and then I'll be back to see all you fuckers again! But thanks a mill lads for letting me steal your girl for the final song of the night."

The stage went black and Andrea heard the first few drumbeats of Oli's best-known song, then a spotlight illuminated and Andrea sucked in a breath as Luna went full-on rock princess and the crowd loved it as she gave a Dave Grohl worthy performance and fitted in with the band.

She must have looked worried because Declan swept her hair from her face. "One-time deal. Oli knows we'd fight him to keep her. But she needed this."

They partied until the early hours and later, as they lay in bed in their rented camper van, Andrea traced her fingers up and down Declan's arm as he slept, the pressure and exhaustion of the day wearing him out so much that he had fallen asleep the moment his head hit the pillow.

Andrea made to get out of bed, unable to sleep so she made herself a cup of tea and sat looking out the window, unable to believe just how happy she was. After the success of Heartache Melody, the job offers were pouring in and Andrea had been tempted by a few but in the end, she knew that any job that took her too far from Declan and the band wasn't worth it.

The weekend passed in a blur and then they were home, with Noah and Charlie heading off back for a new race and Andrea was looking at some offices for Rebel PR's Cork office. Every night she came home to Declan and she was surprised at how blissfully happy the normality of it made her feel.

They'd even had both families over for dinner, with her dad taking Declan outside to have a word, and she rolled her eyes when they both came back in, like deals were made and that was that.

Of course, Rhys was the only one absent, and it hurt her but the band was taking a few weeks off before they put the finishing touches to their album so hopefully, she could persuade her brother to give her an hour to hash things out.

Declan came over and wrapped his arms around her from behind. "You good?"

Andrea turned in his arms and cupped the back of his neck. "I am. I really am?"

Declan bent to kiss her and his brother's cat called at them but Declan flipped them off without taking his gaze from hers. "Any intentions to run?"

"None at all. Unless you want to chase me?" Andrea said the second part in a private whisper as Declan's gaze turned molten.

"I've booked us a holiday. We need a week away from Cork and the media just to be us, Declan and Andi. Plus, I'm getting hard just thinking about you in that tiny bikini I just bought you."

Andrea slapped him hard on the chest and Declan just grinned, stealing another kiss from her as well as the last piece of her heart that had held her back. Their love story had been one of out-of-tune timing and badly written song lyrics that had suddenly become classical and lyrical and the perfect blend of melody and rhyme.

Winking, Andrea crooked her finger at Declan and when he leaned in, she whispered. "Maybe I'll just go swimming naked. I've always wanted to skinny dip."

Declan growled before he kissed her again, telling her that he loved her with his lips and when they broke apart, Andrea placed a hand where Declan's heart was and told him, with no hint of restraint or uncertainty that she loved him too.

"I could change the flights and we could leave tonight. You'll be naked for most of it so it's not like you'll need to pack. A week of no interruptions, no work, and a naked Andi at my mercy. Sounds like fucking heaven."

Andrea's heart was fit to burst and she realized that just like Charlie had said, no matter how much hurt there had been, she wouldn't change the start of their story at all because here and now, life was pretty perfect and she was looking forward to seeing what the future had in store for them.

Her running shoes were officially retired once and for all.

THE END

The Rebel County Universe Stories continue in
Strings Attached (Rebel Rock Book 2)

Find More Rebel Stories On Kindle Vella

All Or Nothing is the second novel in the Rebel Racers Trilogy. Rebel Racers is part of the Rebel County Universe which will span at least four different businesses, with intersecting timelines, and characters popping up when you least expect them.

The Rebel Racers Trilogy
>**Available Now:**
>Adrenaline Junkie (Rebel Racers Book 1)
>All or Nothing (Rebel Racers Book 2)

The Rebel Rock Trilogy
>**Available Now:**
>Centre Stage (Rebel Rock Book 1)
>**Coming Soon:**
>Strings Attached (Rebel Rock Book 2)

Coming Soon:
    Rebel Ink Trilogy
    Rebel Books Trilogy

Playlists

Andrea

Billie Eilish - Halley's Comet

Billie Eilish - Happier Than Ever

Mosh Party - Do My Thing

Sody - Bitch (I Said It)

Joel Corry - OUT OUT (feat. Charli XCX & Saweetie)

Dylan - Someone Else

GAYLE - abcdefu (angrier)

Cami Petyn - Psycho Bitch

LYRA - Lose My Mind

Adele - Easy On Me

Wild Youth - Can't Say No

Halsey - I am not a woman, I'm a god

Leah Kate - F U Anthem (Fuck You Anthem)

Avril Lavigne - Bite Me

Dermot Kennedy - Rome

Adele - Hometown Glory

Halsey - You should be sad

Lauren Spencer-Smith - Fingers Crossed

Ella Eyre - Together

GAYLE - ur just horny

Adele - Oh My God

Anne-Marie - Kiss My (Uh Oh)

Ciara Fox - The Parting Glass

Jessie Ware - Alone

David Gray - This Year's Love

Piano Players Tribute - Look After You - Instrumental

Paramore - The Only Exception

Tokio Myers - Bloodstream

Sheryl Crow - The First Cut Is The Deepest

Felix Jaehn - Rain In Ibiza

Declan

Death From Above 1979 - Modern Guy - grandson remix

grandson - thoughts & prayers

The Regrettes - Stop and Go

FINNEAS - A Concert Six Months From Now

NOISY - Rock 'n' Roll Raver

Macklemore - Next Year (feat. Windser)

Ed Sheeran - Bad Habits

David Guetta - If You Really Love Me (How Will I Know) - David Guetta & MORTEN Future Rave Remix

MEDUZA - Tell It To My Heart

grandson - In Over My Head

Kasabian - ALYGATYR

Five Finger Death Punch - Bad Company

Benson Boone - GHOST TOWN

Sigala - Melody

The Weeknd - How Do I Make You Love Me?

Sueco - Loser

You Me At Six - Voicenotes

Jax Jones - Where Did You Go?

Liam Gallagher - Everything's Electric

Madism - Pumped Up Kicks

Hozier - Someone New

Lewis Capaldi - Someone You Loved

Example - All Night - Extended Club Version

Years & Years - Sanctify
Shouse - Love Tonight - David Guetta Remix
Sam Fender - Seventeen Going Under
Bring Me The Horizon - Can You Feel My Heart
You Me At Six - Take on the World
The National - Never Tear Us Apart
Ed Sheeran - Bloodstream

ACKNOWLEDGMENTS

None of this would be possible without an amazing team supporting me! Many thanks to:

Publishing House: CTP Publishing
Cover design: Gem Promotions
Interior Formating: Gem Promotions

———

And as always:
Thank you to all the readers!
Whether this is your first book by me or you've been with me for years! I only get to do this because of you, and I am eternally grateful to each and every one of you who took a chance on this Irish author.

About the Author

Susan Harris is a writer from Cork, Ireland and when she's not torturing her readers with heart-wrenching plot twists or killer cliffhangers, she's probably getting some new book related ink, binging her latest TV or music obsession, or with her nose in a book.

Susan LOVES connecting with her fans!
www.susanharrisauthor.com

Also by Susan Harris

The Ever Chace Chronicles

Skin & Bones, book 1

Collateral Damage, book 2

Smoke & Mirrors, book 3

Night of the Hunter, book 4

Never Back Down, book 5

Shortcut to the Grave, book 6

Arsonist's Lullaby, book 7

Of Gods & Monsters, book 8

———

Shattered Memories

———

Defy the Stars

A Tale of Two Houses, book 1

Until Death Do Us Part, book 2

In Defiance of the Stars, book 3

The Sanguine Crown

Chaos Theory, book 1

Butterfly Effect, book 2

Wicked Game, book 3

Burn Notice, book 4

Fight Song, book 5

The Sicarius Security Series

Kiss Of Death, book 1

Leap Of Faith, book 2

Visions Of Destiny, book 3